A Forever Friend

A Forever Friend

Angela Elwell Hunt

Tyndale House Publishers, Inc.
Wheaton, Illinois

Library of Congress Catalog Card Number 90-71569
ISBN 0-8423-0462-2
Copyright © 1991 by Angela Elwell Hunt
Front cover illustration copyright © 1991 by Ron Mazellan
All rights reserved
Printed in the United States of America

99 98 97 96 95 94 93 92 91
 9   8   7   6   5   4   3   2   1

Important People in My Life, by Cassie Perkins

1. **Glen Perkins**, my dad. ♥♥♥♥♥.
   A systems analyst at Kennedy Space Center, and my favorite singer. Handsome, even if balding. Now separated from my Mom and living in a condo.

2. **Claire Perkins**, my mom. ♥♥♥♥♥.
   An interior decorator who works at home. Since Dad left, she's pinching pennies, big time. She cries a lot. I hate it when she does.

3. **Max Brian Perkins**, my brother. ♥♥♥♥♥!
   What can you say about a little brother who's cute, smart, helpful and never (well, almost never) a pest? Max lives with Dad in the condo. Probably the worst thing about our family's separation is that I only get to see Max on weekends.

4. **Suki Buki Perkins**, my Chinese pug. ♥♥♥♥♥♥♥!
   'Nuff said.

5. **Andrea Milford**, my best friend. ♥♥♥♥.
   I'd give her five hearts, but I guess I should save those for family. She's cute, athletic, and better at almost everything than I am, but I like her anyway. Sometimes, though, she can be a real jerk. Why do your best friends make the best enemies?

6. **Chip McKinnon**, the cutest guy in school. ♥♥♥♥♥.
   He gets five hearts because *if* we get married someday, he'll be family, too. I never thought I'd stand a chance with him, but ever since singing with me in our school's production of *Oklahoma!* Chip's been one of my best friends.

1

Right before our final song, one of the other kids in the cast passed a note into my hand: "There are VIPs in the audience, so do your best."

I recognized the handwriting of Mr. Williams, our director. But who were the VIPs, and why did Mr. Williams have the note passed to me?

I didn't have time to think any more about it. The music for our final number began, so I slipped the note into my skirt pocket and, with the forty or so other kids in the production cast of Astronaut Junior High, I whirled around and sang and square-danced to the encore from *Oklahoma!* until I was breathless. And I didn't do it just for the VIPs, whoever they were. I did it for Mom, Dad, Max, and me.

The applause crashed like a wave on the beach and just kept coming. Mr. Williams pushed me and Chip back out onto the stage to take our bows for our solos. "Encore! Encore!" I could hear my dad yelling from the audience, and on the other side of the crowd I could see my brother, Max, and my mother, clapping and whistling like crazy.

Chip grabbed my hand, and we bowed again. While we stood there, feeling a little silly, I looked through the crowd for anyone who might be a Very Important Person. But no one stood out.

Behind us, the entire cast spilled out into the crowd, and in the confusion, Chip held tightly to my hand. "Cassie Perkins, you were awesome. I knew you would be."

"I couldn't have done it without you," I answered, squeezing his hand. I meant it. It was Chip who had kept me going during the rough weeks of rehearsal.

I wanted to stand on our makeshift stage forever. We had all worked hard on the musical, and it had been a success. But most importantly, I had finally unveiled the secret no one had ever guessed—Cassie Perkins was not just the ordinary quiet girl everyone knew. I was a singer! I had the heart of a performer, and for the first time I had heard applause meant for *me*.

The stage had only been a taped-off area of the cafeteria floor, and now that people were milling around, it had become an ordinary floor again. It was time to come back to earth. Dad and his date came up to me first, but Mom and Max were right behind him. The situation was a little awkward, especially since my parents' divorce wasn't even final yet, but Dad just smiled and said he was really proud of me and he'd see me next weekend. It was Max's weekend to stay with Mom and me, so Mom hugged me, said she was proud of me, and asked where my things were. It was time to go home.

Mom was quiet on the way home. Maybe she was upset because she saw Dad with a date, but I wished she'd forget about Dad and talk about the show. I had worked really hard to surprise her and wanted her to be, well, floored. Amazed. Stupefied. She acted as though it were no big deal to have a daughter star in the school musical.

Max didn't say anything at all, but I could tell he was as proud and impressed as a nine-year-old boy could be. He wore his "I told you so" expression all the way home, and every now and then he'd look over at me and nod. Boy, a girl could get carried away by all the enthusiasm in this family.

I just sat and watched the street lights go by. I imagined that every one of them was a spotlight that would some day shine on me. After all, the VIPs had seen me, and I was good. I knew I was good because Chip McKinnon had said so, and he's my best friend who's a boy. (Not a boyfriend, if you know what I mean.) But more than that, I knew I had done a good job because I had *connected* with the music, the audience, and the other singers, and for two hours I had been in heaven.

"Max," I said as I turned and leaned toward the backseat, "what did you think about my solo on 'Many a Blue Moon'? Was it playful enough? I was so nervous, I couldn't tell if I got it right."

"It was great," he said. "Cassie, you were the best thing in the show."

"Now, Max," Mom interrupted, "let's not give Cassie a big head, OK? She'll be impossible to live with."

Was that it? Was Mom afraid I'd become conceited?

Max rolled his eyes. "You really were the best," he whispered.

"Thanks."

I fell into bed that night thinking I was too excited to sleep and more tired than I'd ever been all at the same time. Suki, my pug, jumped up to her usual place at the foot of my bed, and I raised up on my elbows to look down at her. "It was great, Suki," I said. "Some VIPs were there. Maybe they were from a record company or a movie studio." Boy, wouldn't Mom be surprised when Universal Pictures or RCA called tomorrow to offer me a contract! Or maybe the VIPs weren't in movies or records, but were politicians. I could be invited to sing at the mayor's office, the governor's mansion, even the White House! Or maybe they were reporters. My face could be on the cover of *People* as America's newest singing sensation!

Before turning out the light, I looked around

my room. Everything looked the same—my posters and books and collection of ceramic frogs (the *People* photographers would like that)—but I felt totally different. Anything was possible now, with a little help from a VIP!

"Cassie," Mom called the next morning, "it's your turn to do the vacuuming. Get up, get dressed, and help me clean this house!"

I groaned. The glow was gone. Obviously, I wasn't going to get any star treatment, not even an extra hour's sleep. I felt like Cinderella after the ball, except that I didn't even have a leftover slipper to mark the occasion. But I did have something! I pulled my square-dancing skirt from the heap of clothes on the floor and pulled the note from the pocket. "There are VIPs in the audience, so do your best," I read aloud. I'd done my best, so what would happen now?

The phone rang, and I heard Max answer it in the kitchen. Was it the VIPs already?

"Cassie, it's Andrea," Max yelled.

"Coming!" I jumped out of bed and lunged for my phone.

"Where'd you run off to last night?" Andrea sounded amazingly energetic after our busy night. "I wanted to come over and congratulate the star, but you had, like, vanished. Chip and his parents were looking for you, too."

"Sorry," I said, "Mom just wanted to get out of there."

"Were your parents surprised? What'd they say?"

"They liked it, sure. Yeah, they were surprised."

"My parents were really impressed," Andrea rattled on. "They loved my square-dance routines, they thought Chip was darling, and they couldn't believe you! My mom wanted to know why you've been hiding your talent all these years, and my dad said you were the best singer to ever come out of Canova Cove."

"Tell your mom I've been too busy keeping up with you," I teased, thinking of all the times Andrea had put me to shame in gymnastics, tap, and ballet lessons. "And tell your dad thanks. By the way, did you hear anything about VIPs there last night?"

Andrea laughed. "No. Who were they?"

"I don't know. I just wondered."

"Well, now that things are back to normal, would you and Max like to come over and spend the day with us on the boat?"

Spending the day on the Milfords' boat sounded wonderful, but I didn't want to leave the house, especially not today. The VIPs might call. Besides, ever since my parents separated, it hasn't been easy to get away on weekends. "You know how it is, Andrea," I said hesitantly. "It's Max's weekend here, and I think Mom would be hurt if we left."

"That's OK. I understand," Andrea answered, but she didn't really. She couldn't. Her parents lived together.

"Well, have fun. Don't get sunburned, OK?"

Before the separation, Max and I spent every

Saturday afternoon snacking in front of the Creature Feature on TV. Dad would work on the lawn or tinker on his computer, and Mom would go to her tennis lesson. But in the months A.D. (After the Divorce), Dad was gone and Mom cleared her Saturday afternoons to spend time with us.

This "spending time" stuff was not always great. Even though she's a good interior decorator, Mom's on a tight budget, and spending time means *not* spending money. One weekend she took us to Disney World, but that blew her budget for the year, so now we pretty much stay home.

Today we were making homemade pizza—or at least trying to. "I know that recipe's in here somewhere," Mom muttered, searching through her dusty cookbooks on the lowest kitchen shelf. "Pizza crust isn't all that complicated, is it, Max?"

Max shook his head. "It's just a combination of flour and water, unless you want to add a spice," he said.

"I had a pizza once with Parmesan cheese in the dough," I added, trying to be helpful. "It was good."

"We'll skip the cheese," Mom said, brushing off her knees and standing up. "Max, you can figure out how to make crust, can't you? And for the sauce, Cassie, just open up a can of tomato sauce and throw in some oregano. We don't have pepperoni, but there are some hot dogs we can slice for the topping."

Ugh. It didn't sound very good, but Max had already tied on an apron and was measuring flour and water with the seriousness of a rocket scientist.

An hour later, Max had spilled flour all over the counter as he spun circles of dough over his head counting the revolutions per minute, and I had thoroughly botched up the sauce (oregano and tomato sauce is *not* all there is to it). Mom is not a cook, so she couldn't complain, but she is the original neat freak, so she gave us a tired look and left the kitchen. "Just clean it up," she sighed as she left, "and I'll call the pizza delivery man. I just hope it doesn't cost too much."

2

While we ate the real pizza, I realized there was another reason I was glad I stayed home instead of going with Andrea. I would have worried about Mom.

Mom isn't herself these days; she worries a lot, mostly about money. Dad sends a support check every month, but it's not much because Max lives with Dad. Since Mom and Dad are each raising one kid, things are supposed to be fair. But Dad is a systems analyst at Kennedy Space Center, and he makes a lot more than Mom does at her interior decorating business.

Last week Dad's support check was two days late. Just before the check came I caught Mom walking through the house in a daze, touching the drapes and furniture like someone who's being deported to Siberia.

"What are you doing?" I asked.

"We'll lose it all if the check doesn't come," she said, running her fingers over the piano keys. "Without the check, I can't pay the mortgage. If I can't pay the mortgage, we'll have to move. If we move, you'll have to go to a new school."

I was sorry I'd asked. If I had to go to a new school, I'd lose touch with all my friends, especially my best friends, Andrea and Chip. No wonder she was depressed.

"Your father is so irresponsible." She moved on and practically hugged the blue wing chair she'd had reupholstered to match the wallpaper. "Doesn't he care about you at all? How can he be such a thoughtless jerk?"

I couldn't stand to hear her cut my dad down. "Let me go see if the mail has come," I offered. "I'm sure the check will be here today."

It was. Mom snapped out of her weird mood and was fine again, but I've decided to ask Dad to please, please, *please* mail the check on time.

I guess I should be glad my parents have worked out their problems as well as they have. They don't ever really fight—at least they don't hit each other—and we have our visitation schedules worked out so that I spend one weekend with Dad and Max in their condo; the next weekend Max comes home with Mom and me. Dad is into spending time together, too. When we're at his place, we usually lie around on the beach and watch for goofy tourists with their sandals and socks and cameras.

All things considered, we probably see more of our parents since they separated than we did before. Max says this is all part of a guilt trip, though, and soon things will be back to normal. I do miss seeing Max every day.

After we finished our pizza, Mom left the kitchen to go fold laundry, grumbling that Dad didn't do his fair share of Max's dirty clothes. I looked over at the whiz kid, still in his apron.

"Any new experiments? Are you still working on the cure for cancer?"

Max nodded, and his brown eyes were serious. "Of course I don't have the research facilities I need, but I'm developing a few theories. In the meantime, I'm working on a new project."

I couldn't stop a smile, remembering how Max used to conduct his experiments all over the house. The real fun was seeing his outfits. Max always dressed to suit the occasion.

"Are you still growing algae?"

"Yes." He nodded. "And I'm very close to a breakthrough on something. Do you remember the time I baked algae cookies?"

"Yuck! Of course! I ate one."

"That's precisely the problem with algae in human food. Humans just aren't ready to accept algae as a nutritious food additive."

"So?"

"Animals are. My gerbils have been eating it all along and are doing very nicely. I've even developed some small algae bits that I bake in flour. I've been feeding it to the sea gulls on the beach."

I crinkled my nose in disgust. "Do they like it?"

"They love it." Max beamed. "I've got them trained. When I come home from school, they're sitting on the balcony railing, waiting for dinner."

I slipped off my kitchen stool. "I'll bet Dad is proud of you."

"Actually, no." The gleam of excitement left his eyes. "He told me to stop because the birds are—well, you know how birds are. The balcony is a mess."

I giggled. I could just see Max on his hands and knees, in a decontamination outfit and mask, scrubbing away bird droppings. "Well, good luck in finding another animal to experiment on."

"That's just it." Max leaned over the counter on his elbows. "I was hoping you'd let me feed some of my algae bits to Suki."

"No way!" I started to back out of the room. "She's an old dog, and I won't let you feed her anything experimental."

"But—"

"Forget it, Max."

At five o'clock, the VIPs still hadn't called, so I guessed they took Saturdays off. I picked up the phone and called Andrea, hoping the Milfords were back from the beach. They were.

"How was the water?" I asked Andrea.

"Fine," she answered. "How was your day at home?"

"Boring," I laughed, "except for the mess we made in the kitchen. It looked like that scene from 'I Love Lucy' where Lucy's dough explodes all over the ceiling."

"I met a guy on the beach who goes to Astronaut High," Andrea volunteered. "Can you believe we'll be there in just four months?"

"I think I'll miss junior high," I mumbled.

"You're crazy," Andrea said, snapping her gum in my ear. "There are more hunks per square foot in high school. I can't wait."

"I can," I sighed. Compared to the excitement of last night, even this conversation was boring. "I'll talk to you later, OK? Bye."

I hung up abruptly, but I just didn't want to talk about leaving Astronaut Junior High. I had spent so many hours in the choir room with my friends and Mr. Williams. When things got so crazy a few months ago when my parents split up, it was the production of *Oklahoma!* that pulled me through. I knew I'd miss school a lot, unless, of course, I was leaving it to go make a movie or something.

When the dismissal bell rang on Monday afternoon, I rushed toward the choir room. I just had to find out something about the VIPs. The other cast members were glad they could go home at the normal time instead of staying late for another rehearsal, but I flew through the hall and yanked open the choir room door.

The big rehearsal room was empty, but I could see the top of Mr. Williams's bald head through the glass on his office door. I knocked.

"Why, Cassie, come in," he said, smiling and looking up from his grade book. "I haven't had a chance to congratulate you on your fine performance Friday night. You did a great job, a really fine job."

"Thanks, Mr. Williams, but none of us could have done it without you." He had been an excellent coach and teacher.

"Nonsense. You have a talent that's easy to work with. You surprised the whole school, young lady, and you even surprised me."

"Surprised you?"

"Oh, I know I've heard you rehearse day after day, but something happened to you that night. You came alive under that spotlight, and you didn't get swallowed up in jitters and stage fright like a lot of kids do. You absolutely bloomed."

He seemed to be studying me, and I felt a little uncomfortable, so I laughed and tried to change the subject. I was so anxious to know about the VIPs, I could have screamed.

"It was like I was a different person out there," I said. "Someone new and exciting. I thought it'd be fun to do something like that all the time, even professionally."

Mr. Williams laughed and leaned back in his chair. "I'm glad to hear you say that,

Cassie. You have a unique talent, and I'd like to see you use it all the time."

Was this it? I held my breath.

Mr. Williams tapped his pencil on his desk thoughtfully. "Are you familiar with the Central Florida School for Performing Arts?"

I shook my head.

"Well, it's a private secondary school near the edge of town. I'll be honest—I've hesitated to mention it to my students because it's very difficult to get into. But there they teach not only what you need to get your high school diploma, but also music, dance, acting, and vocal performance. It's a very disciplined routine, but you've already shown me that you can handle discipline."

"It sounds great." Wasn't he ever going to mention the VIPs? Did this school have something to do with it?

Mr. Williams went on. "The students go to classes from eight until two, then they rehearse from three until five every day. There is no football team, sports, or student government. But there is a jazz band, a drama troupe, dance recitals, and more performances than a public school could ever offer."

He paused and leaned on his desk, crossing his arms. "There are only one or two openings per grade each year for new students, and applicants from all over the state apply for those openings. But I'd like to recommend you for next year."

I cleared my throat and pulled out the note. "Did the VIPs have anything to do with that school?"

Mr. Williams seemed confused. He read the note and looked up at me. "No," he said, turning red, "the VIPs were personal friends of mine. But what about the school, Cassie? Are you interested?"

I couldn't answer. Me go to a school like that? Sing, dance, act, and perform every day? It sounded too good to be true.

"There is a charge for tuition," Mr. Williams said, interrupting my thoughts, "but I want you to go home and seriously talk to your parents about this. I think you are the kind of student they want, and I think it is the kind of school you're going to need if you really want to do something with your talent."

I was thinking, and Mr. Williams raised an eyebrow. "Did I assume too much? Do you want to do something with your talent?"

"Oh, yes," I said, nodding. "More than anything!"

He smiled. "Then talk to your parents. The tuition is five thousand dollars per semester, which seems expensive, but you can live at home so you won't have to pay room and board. You'd be getting a lot of instruction for the money."

"OK." I turned to leave and stopped by his door to ask one more question. "Mr. Williams?"

"Yes?"

"Do you have any personal friends in the movie business?"

"Why, no," he said, smiling. "Why do you ask?"

"Nothing," I answered. "Just curious."

3

Now that I'd talked to Mr. Williams, I realized the VIPs were probably just ordinary people, friends of his. And—I blushed when I thought about it—that note probably wasn't intended for me alone. Mr. Williams probably wrote it and sent it around so *everyone* would do a good job. The Very Important People could have even been our own parents! How stupid I had been! But it was OK. At least I hadn't told anyone about waiting around the house for *People* magazine to call. Besides, even if I wasn't ready for a record company now, I *could* be after going to the School for Performing Arts.

When I told Mom I wanted to go to a private school that would cost five thousand dollars per semester, she hit the roof. "Cassiopeia Perkins, you've flipped," she said over our dinner of frozen diet entrees. "I don't know where I'm going to get the money to buy your summer bathing suit, and you sit here and tell me you want ten thousand dollars for one year at some fancy schmancy school."

"It's a performance arts school," I whispered, trying to explain.

"You want to sing?" She laughed. "Fine, sing all you want! But sing here. It's free."

My penny-pinching mother was going to be about as open-minded as a brick. "You want to dance?" she continued, pointing at me with her fork. "Didn't I send you to ballet and tap and all that when you were little? We could afford it then, but we couldn't even afford *that* stuff now. Where's the future in it? I will not let you waste your time dreaming about something that will never give you a skill. Girls need a marketable skill, Cassie, because you've got to be able to support yourself. Come back to the real world, honey. Don't let one little show go to your head."

One little show! It wasn't little to me.

"I *am* thinking about the real world, Mom," I tried to explain. "I just want to see if I have a chance to make it as a performer. I may not even get into the performance school; then I'll know I could never cut it as a professional. But I've just got to try."

"Honey, I don't want to hear another word about it," Mom said, dismissing the idea as easily as she skipped over the peas in her beef stew. "Even if you did qualify, I simply can't afford the tuition. Even if your father agreed to pay half, I couldn't afford the other half. Some things just weren't meant to be, Cassie, and this is one of them."

"I won't know that unless I try," I mumbled.

Mom ignored me and carefully buttered a slice of bread. "I think I'll call Mr. Williams and give him a piece of my mind. He's filled your head with all these foolish thoughts and got you all excited about going to some overrated school when you were perfectly content to attend Astronaut High like everybody else."

"It's not his fault, Mom." I rose to his defense. "Can't you see that this is something I just need to try? If I pass the audition, *then* I'll worry about finding the money."

"You've got ten thousand dollars under your mattress?" Mom looked at me. "You've got a money tree planted in the backyard?"

"No." I stirred my beef stew. I hated it when she was sarcastic.

"If you don't audition, you won't get your hopes up. But what if you should pass the entrance audition and then have to withdraw? That wouldn't be fair to someone else who could have won that spot."

She reached out and smoothed my hair. "Honey, if money were no object, I'd let you go in an instant. I know you would enjoy it, and I'm sure it's a fine school. You could always learn to do something practical in college. But money is a problem, and I don't want you to get hurt because your hopes were crushed."

I opened my mouth to speak, but she shook her head again. "I'm sorry, Cassie, but that is the end of this discussion. That school is simply out of our reach, and you're going to have to get by with what we can afford. Sign up for the high school choir at Astronaut and work on your ballet with Andrea. That's better than nothing."

Nothing. A big, fat zero. That's what I accomplished tonight, I told myself as I cleared the table. *I probably ruined my chances forever.* But I still had hope. I could still ask Dad.

I could hardly wait for Friday afternoon. It was my turn to spend the weekend with Max and Dad at their condo on the beach, and when Dad finally picked me up, I was about to burst with my news. Mom had let me down, but Dad wouldn't.

Dad took Max and me to a little Italian restaurant with red-checked tablecloths and cozy little booths. "Well, gypsy girl, you really wowed us at your show last week," Dad said, sliding into a booth. "I never dreamed you could sing like that."

"I get it from you," I said, smiling at him. "Remember how you always used to sing to me?" I clasped my hands in front of me and warbled, "My Wild Irish Rose" just the way Dad used to. Several people turned around to stare at us.

Dad laughed and covered his face with the

menu. The waitress chose that moment to come to take our order, and Dad tried to explain why he was red-faced and why Max and I were giggling.

"We have a budding singer here," he said, pointing to me.

"Oh no, we have a great singer here," I said, pointing back at him, "but he only sings in the shower."

The waitress raised an eyebrow and looked at Dad's hand. When she didn't see a wedding ring, she fluttered her lashes. "I'd like to hear you sometime," she crooned.

Dad just looked at me and Max. "Pizza tonight? Or lasagna? What'll it be?"

We both ordered lasagna, so Dad did, too, and the waitress took our menus and walked away without any other comments or flirty smiles.

I took a deep breath. It was now or never. "You know you really are a good singer, Dad," I said. "You should sing more often."

Dad smiled, and his dark eyes danced with mischief. "No way," he said, pulling my hair. "I'll leave that to you."

"OK," I said cautiously. "That's something I'd like to talk to you about."

"Shoot," Dad said. But the waitress came back with our drinks, and I waited until she had passed them out and gone before saying anything else.

"Mr. Williams says the Central Florida School for Performing Arts has a few vacancies for next year. He thinks I could pass the entrance audition. I've thought about it, and I'd really like to go for it."

Dad chuckled. "Gypsy girl, I can't think of a bigger waste of your time." He took a sip of his tea. "Singing, acting, dancing, and all that—it's only a waste of time and energy."

I couldn't believe it. Were he and Mom reading from the same script? I had thought Dad would understand. After all, he has talent and could have been a fine singer if he had tried. Why was he discouraging me?

"I don't think it's a waste, Dad," I said gently, trying not to start an argument. "I think I'd really like to someday be a professional performer. I'd at least like to try."

He kept smiling, but his eyes darkened. "Cassie, you can take my word for it. Just because you have talent, even an exceptional talent, doesn't mean you can cut it in show business. Singers are a dime a dozen, gypsy girl, and I don't want you to be any part of it."

I was probably asking for trouble, but I couldn't resist asking: "How do you know?"

Dad frowned and pressed his lips together. "I know," he said flatly. Then he leaned back and patted Max on the shoulder. "Use the family genes instead to make some intellectual progress. Be like Max here. Find a good academic college and go into research or medicine or education. Use your brains, for heaven's sake. I know you've got them!"

That hurt. Neither of my parents had ever actually compared me to Max, at least out loud, but I've always wondered if they wanted me to be more like the boy genius. Max is such a brain, they probably think I've been intellectually loafing all these years. But I just don't have what Max has! We may have the same genes, but they didn't come out in the same package.

Even Max was surprised. "Gee, Dad," he muttered, "Cassie just doesn't like the same stuff I do. It's not her fault."

"Well, Cassie needs to begin to think seriously about the future." Dad took his arm from around Max and leaned his elbows on the table. His dark eyes were serious. "Cassie, you'll be entering high school at the end of the summer, and it is not too soon to begin planning for college. You need to take college prep classes, a foreign language, chemistry, advanced algebra, and trig—don't waste your time with all this choir stuff."

It was useless to argue with Dad once he got an idea into his head, so I just nodded while my eyes filled with tears of frustration. Just because he and Max had super-brains, why did Dad expect me to be like them?

Dad brought his girlfriend, Julie Smith, over to his condo later that night, and we all sat around and made polite and boring small talk until I thought I'd go crazy. It wasn't fun for Julie, either, and after about fifteen minutes Dad stood up and announced that he and Julie were going out for ice cream. Did we want them to bring us anything?

No. Max and I were glad to have the place to ourselves. As soon as Dad and Julie left, Max and I raided the kitchen for munchies and spread whatever we could find out on the kitchen table.

"I can't believe he doesn't keep a supply of Twinkies for you," I said, rummaging in all the most likely hiding places.

"He did at first," Max said, "but I ate them so fast he limits me now to twelve packages every two weeks. They only last a couple of days."

"You poor, deprived child." I rumpled his curly hair. "How can you survive without Twinkies?"

"I manage. I have a hiding place." Max reached into the oven and pulled out a brown paper bag. "Dad never uses the oven." From the bag he pulled out two packages of chocolate pastries. "These chocolate Ring-a-Dings are almost as good as Twinkies. I pick them up on my way home from school."

"Yum. I'll pour us some milk." We sat and dipped our Ring-a-Dings into milk at the kitchen table. I was glad I had a chance to talk to Max alone. "What am I going to do?" I asked, dipping a big hunk of chocolate into my milk. "I want to go to that performance school more than anything in the world."

"It really means that much to you?"

"Yes. Mom won't talk about it because it costs money. Dad, who has money, won't talk about it because he thinks I'm wasting my share of the family intellect. He just doesn't understand that I didn't get a full share of brains."

"Come on, Cassie, you're not stupid."

"No, but I'm no whiz kid, either. That's your job, and you can have it. Why can't they see that I'm just average? I'm never going to win the Nobel Prize."

"So what do you want to do? Sing?"

I gazed dreamily out the sliding door beyond the beach where the ocean wind whipped the waves. "I want to go to the performance arts school and really develop my talent. Someday I'll go to New York and be cast in a Broadway play. I'll make records and give concerts and travel all over the world."

I stopped for a moment and realized how silly I must sound to practical Max. "But with both Mom and Dad against me, I don't have a chance."

Max dunked another Ring-a-Ding into his milk. "How does Dad know so much about show business?"

I shrugged. "I don't know."

Max leaned forward, that don't-you-ever-wonder-why look in his eye. "Do you think Dad has ever tried to sing?"

I frowned. "I always figured he was more interested in space than in music."

Max shook his head. "He wasn't always interested in space. Dad told me that he didn't start thinking about space until he was fifteen. That was in 1961, when the Russians first put men into orbit. So maybe he tried music before then."

I shook my head. "I just can't imagine him singing anywhere but in the shower."

"That's because you've only known him for thirteen years. Maybe he was a singer when he was a kid, but later he figured that music was a waste of time."

"Maybe you have an overactive imagination," I answered, swallowing the last bite of my Ring-a-Ding. "And if you eat any more of that junk food, you'll be sick."

"OK, I'm done," Max said, smacking his lips. "But I'm going to do some thinking. I'm sure there's a reason why Dad is so set against music. It isn't like him to be against something for no logical reason."

"He left Mom, didn't he?" I muttered. "And I still haven't heard a logical reason for that."

4

For weeks I had been dreaming about what it would be like to walk into school with everyone whispering, "Did you hear that Cassie Perkins is a great singer?" but now that my dream had come true, all I could think of was how to convince Mom and Dad to let me audition for the arts school. *Oklahoma!* had been great, but now that I knew about the performance arts school, I wasn't satisfied.

Andrea and Chip were waiting for me on one of the concrete picnic tables outside the choir room. "Hi, Cassie," Chip said, and for a split second I forgot about the school and all I could think of was that it had been an eternity since I had last looked into those blue eyes of his.

But I shook my head and came back to earth. "Hi, you guys. What's up?"

"Not much," Andrea said with a shrug,

looking around as everyone straggled onto the school grounds. "It's sort of sad that we've got to go back to regular school, isn't it?"

Chip laughed. "I'm ready for regular school. All that square dancing in the show had my feet tied up in knots."

Andrea and I laughed, too, remembering how much the guys had resisted square dancing. It wasn't a very macho thing to do, but they had done a good job.

"You know," I said slowly, "things don't have to go back to regular school. Mr. Williams said he thought I had a chance to make it into the Central Florida School for Performing Arts."

"What?" Andrea was startled. "You'd change schools?"

"Wouldn't you?" I asked.

Unless I was imagining things, Chip looked more hurt than surprised. He looked down at the ground for a minute, then echoed Andrea: "You'd change schools?"

"Why would you want to do that?" Andrea asked. "We're almost to Astronaut High, and you know how we've talked about going to football games, trying out for cheerleading, and remember—" She leaned closer to whisper in my ear. "More hunks per square foot!"

"Cheerleading is your thing, Andrea, not mine," I answered, shifting my books from one hip to the other. "I've always tried out with you just to keep you company. And I really don't care much about football games."

"What about Astronaut High's drama program?" Chip offered. "You know they do even bigger productions than we do here. And you're so good, Cassie, I know you could get practically any part you wanted."

"Thanks, Chip, but I want to *concentrate* on singing, not just do it once a year. I'm dying to audition for the school, but Mom won't even think about it because we can't afford the tuition, and Dad won't consider it because he thinks music is a waste of time."

I kicked a pebble with my shoe and watched it skitter across the sidewalk. "So as much as I want to go, I guess I'll have to tell Mr. Williams to recommend someone else."

Andrea bit her lip thoughtfully. "I'm against you going to another school, you understand? I can't believe you'd be disloyal to your school and your friends. But I think I know a way you can get into this school, if you really want to go."

"How?"

"A scholarship. My mother's women's club is always raising money for causes, and just last month she mentioned that the school for performance arts has more patrons than any cause in the city. I'm sure there are scholarships available."

"You're kidding." I sat down abruptly on the bench. I had almost resigned myself to not going to the school, not working in New York, not singing on Broadway, and never becoming a star. But suddenly my little ember of hope burst into flame. "A scholarship!" I whispered.

"Yes, and there are work-study programs, too, I'll bet. If you've got the talent, Cassie, they'll find a way to get you enrolled. Why don't you ask Mr. Williams to check it out for you?"

I was through the choir room door in less than ten seconds.

"Scholarships? I'm sure there are scholarships," Mr. Williams said, digging through a stack of papers on his desk. "Just a minute and let me see what I can find here—aha, here it is! For the ninth grade level for next year, there are four openings and one scholarship available—the Constance Hamilton Scholarship. It pays tuition for one student for four years."

Mr. Williams peered over the top of his glasses at me. "Would that help?"

"Would it!" I decided to be honest. "Mr. Williams, I can't go unless I earn a scholarship. My mother said she can't pay the tuition, and my dad says he won't."

"Ummm." Mr. Williams looked down at his paper again. "I don't know what to tell you. If you work hard and pass the entrance audition, I'm sure you'll deserve the scholarship, but I've no way of knowing how they'll award it."

He handed me a folder. "Inside there you'll find a brochure about the school, an application for admission, a list of the school's past productions, and financial aid information. You'll notice they did *Oklahoma!* three years ago." He smiled, leaning back in his chair, and said, "and I know the performance you gave here as leading lady would have been more than welcome in their school."

He leaned forward again and tapped the folder. "Inside there is also a letter about a meeting for interested applicants on June 14. I suggest you and your mother attend. Find out what is required at the audition and go for that scholarship. What do you have to lose?"

I grasped the folder tightly. "OK, I will!"

"And, Cassie, if you need any help, please don't hesitate to call me. I'd be happy to coach you." He took off his glasses and leaned back in his squeaky chair. "I'd be honored if my star pupil was accepted to the Central Florida School for Performing Arts."

I could have kissed him, but I just smiled. "Mr. Williams, you're the greatest."

5

The last two weeks of school seemed dull beyond belief now that *Oklahoma!* was over. There were the usual exams, yearbook signing parties, and long, lazy study halls where more people slept than studied. When June 8 finally rolled around, we turned in our books, cleaned out our lockers, and made promises to stay in touch with practically everyone, even though we knew we wouldn't.

I didn't know if I'd ever see anybody again. What if I actually *did* get into the School for Performing Arts? What if I stayed there for all four years of high school and graduated from there instead of Astronaut High? Andrea and Chip wouldn't be my classmates anymore—a few weeks ago, when Mom was moaning about moving, I thought it would be terrible to go to a different school. But now I wanted it more than anything in the world.

I knew Andrea would always be my friend because we've been best friends since kindergarten. Besides, we live close enough that we can walk to each other's house if we want to. But Chip was a different story.

I found him coming out of the choir room after school. "I thought you might be here to see Mr. Williams," I said, a little awkwardly. "So I thought I'd come by to say good-bye to the best co-star a girl could have."

Chip raised an eyebrow. "That's it? You're just going to say good-bye and walk off?"

I could feel my cheeks burning, and I couldn't think of anything to say. "What else did you want me to say?" I looked down at the ground.

"Come on, let's go sit down." Chip grabbed my elbow and steered me toward the picnic table near the parking lot. Many of the cars and nearly all of the bikes in the bicycle rack were gone.

We sat down, and Chip said, "You know, we might be the last two kids to leave."

I nodded. "Why not? We've probably spent more time here than anyone else." It felt strange to sit at the picnic table without a mountain of books in front of me, so I put my purse in the empty space. I didn't know where I stood with Chip anymore. We had been on sort of a date once, but everyone in school teased us so much about it that we hadn't done anything together since. But we were singing partners in the show, and besides Andrea, Chip was the best, most honest friend I had. He was the only person in the world who had ever told me that God loved me, and he said it so simply and honestly that I believed him.

Chip sat across from me and leaned his head on his hand. "So what are you going to do this summer?"

I shrugged. "I suppose I'll be spending every other weekend with Dad and Max and weekdays helping Mom. She wants me to be the secretary for her interior decorator business—you know, answer the phones and stuff like that." I ran my fingernail over the concrete tabletop. "What will you be doing?"

Chip's eyes lit up. "I'm working as a vet's assistant in the mornings and helping my uncle at his kennel in the afternoons. I start on Monday."

"That's great." Knowing that Chip's passion was dogs, I understood why he was excited. "Sounds like fun."

"Yeah." He looked up, and I noticed again how blue his eyes were. "Are you really going to audition for that music school?"

I hadn't brought it up because I knew Chip didn't really approve of my switching schools. But I wanted to be honest. I nodded. "I found out they offer a scholarship, and I'm going to go for it. I don't know that I'll get it, or even if I'll be accepted, but I won't know unless I try, right? I don't want to be disloyal or anything, but this is something I've just got to do!"

Chip smiled, and I nearly melted with relief. "It's OK, Cassie, nobody thinks you're a traitor or anything. We'll just miss you, that's all."

"I probably won't even make it in."

"Oh, yes, you will," Chip said, nodding. "They'd be dumb to let you get away."

I could feel myself blushing again, so I stretched out a fingernail again to scratch the concrete tabletop. Chip grabbed my hand and looked steadily at me, and, for once, I didn't look away. My hand felt so secure in his.

"Are you going to be so busy auditioning that you won't have any free time this summer?" he asked. "Like maybe sometime we could meet at the mall or something?"

"No," I whispered, then stammered, "I mean, I won't be too busy."

"Good," he said, releasing my hand. "I'll keep in touch."

I had waited until the last day of school to tell Mom about the possibility of a scholarship because it seemed more natural to talk about going to a new school once I had finished with the old one. When I came home, she was in our living room flailing her arms to an exercise video.

"Hi, honey," she called, stopping to stretch out on the carpet. "How was the last day of school?"

"Fine," I said, plopping into my favorite chair, the only one I was allowed to *plop* into. "It was really lazy. I don't know why they bother to have school on the last day."

"Silly," Mom said, panting between abdominal curls. "There has to be a last day, unless you want to go to school forever."

"I guess so." It was now or never. "Mom," I said as I pulled the folded papers Mr. Williams had given me from my purse. "I've got some information here about a scholarship to the performing arts school. Mr. Williams thinks I have a good chance at winning it."

"A scholarship?" She didn't miss a sit-up, but her brows crinkled in thought.

"Yes. It wouldn't cost you a thing because I'd still live at home and the tuition would be paid. I'm going to practice really hard, and Mr. Williams said he'd be glad to coach me for the audition."

The long-legged lady on the exercise video sat up and crossed her legs, so my mother did the same. She pressed her chin to her chest and took a deep breath. "Relax," the lady said, "breathe in through the nose and out through the mouth. Blow those troubles away."

Mom did look relaxed. After a few seconds, she raised her head and looked at me. "That's fine, honey. If you really think you can win a scholarship, go ahead and try. But I just hope you aren't too disappointed if you don't win this thing. Doing a good job is one thing—and I expect you to do the best you can do—but winning a scholarship is something else. There's a lot more involved, and there may be things you aren't able to control."

"It's OK, Mom. I only want to try."

"OK." She closed her eyes and lowered her head. "Just do your best."

I hopped up and gave her a grateful peck on the cheek. Incredible! If only my dad were that easy to convince!

I lay on my bed and whistled for Suki. She used to be able to hop on my bed in one bound, but she's older now, and fatter. Sometimes I have to grab her and heave her onto the bed.

Once she was settled into her usual place at my feet, I put my hands behind my head and thought. Mom was agreeable to the plan, and Mr. Williams was willing to help me. That was all I really needed. Then why did it bother me so much that Dad was still against the idea?

It was the first time I could remember that what *both* my parents said didn't matter. It was a little confusing: I knew I had to go by Mom's rules at her house, and Dad's rules at his condo, but whose rules applied when it was just about me? Who had the final word about school? Mom said she was the "custodial parent" and legally responsible for me, but never before had Mom said it was OK to do something Dad was against.

I reached over to my desk and pulled down the little black notebook I write in. I've been writing in it since fifth grade, and no one ever reads it, unless Mom peeks when I'm out. It's full of songs, poems, and silly pictures that I sketch when I'm in a mood.

I was in a mood, for sure, so I wrote:

You say go,
But he says no,
And I feel woe
In the middle.

He lives up,
And you live down,
And I am stuck
In the middle.

I am here,
But Max is there,
Kids must beware
In the middle.

If I must choose,
Someone will lose,
It's all bad news
In the middle.

I knew that poem wouldn't win any prizes, but I felt better after writing it. A little voice inside me whispered, "Show it to Dad! Make him squirm! He'll let you go to the audition! Even if you don't win the scholarship, he'll feel so bad he'll pay the tuition!"

But I didn't want to play any sneaky little games. I remember once Andrea came to school in an outfit that just the week before her mother said she couldn't have because it was too expensive. "How'd you get it?" I asked. "Did it go on sale?"

Andrea had smiled a sneaky little smile and whispered, "It was easy. I just went up to my dad and said, 'Daddy? Remember those little Easter outfits you used to buy me? I haven't had one since I was your little girl!'"

"You're kidding!" I shook my head. "He bought *that?*"

"Yes." Andrea nodded, biting her lip to stop a giggle. "He not only bought the little girl story, he bought the outfit!"

Somehow I knew Dad had enough guilt to spring for an outfit or two, and maybe there was even enough for him to give in and pay for the performance school. But I just didn't want to use him like that. Since the separation, I'd had enough of people using each other.

6

The Central Florida School for Performing Arts was a two-story brick building with windows only in the stairwells. Mom and I walked into the quiet, carpeted lobby where a message board announced directions: New and Returning Students' Orientation Meeting, Room 200, 7:00 P.M.

"Plush, isn't it?" I whispered to Mom.

"Yes," she whispered back, "but I don't know why we're whispering. This red carpet is louder than both of us!"

I laughed, glad she was in a good mood. We found the staircase up to room 200. The quiet of the lobby was a direct contrast to the activity of this room. Two rows of chairs hugged the walls of the large room, and nervous kids and even more nervous parents were seated in little clumps around the room. In the exact center of the room stood a lectern of polished wood.

Mom and I slipped into two empty seats near the door. I looked around. There were a few kids who looked to be in seventh or eighth grade, and one kid with straight black hair and Coke-bottle glasses. "Look at him," I whispered to Mom, pointing. "He's probably a violin prodigy."

"Don't point," Mom lectured. "And you can't judge a person by their glasses."

All at once I had the feeling that someone was sizing me up, too. I was right. Across the room was a girl, about my age, but unlike me in every other way. I am short and dark-haired, but this girl was a tall, glamorous blonde. She was wearing a sleeveless summer sweater with jeans, and her tan was deep and even. Her sparkling blue eyes reminded me of Chip's, and her absolutely perfect white teeth were smiling at me.

"At least she's friendly," I mumbled, and my mother overheard.

"Who?"

"That girl over there," I nodded with my head.

"Good grief," my mother said, spotting her. "Does Christie Brinkley have a twin sister down here?"

We were both a little surprised when the girl stood up and walked over. "Hello," she said, extending her hand to my mother. "I'm Shalisa McRay."

"Hello," Mom answered. "I'm Claire Perkins and this is my daughter, Cassiop—"

"Cassie," I interrupted. "Just Cassie." Why, oh why, had my father given me that stupid name?

50

"Cassie, as in Cassiopeia, the constellation?" Shalisa asked. "As in Greek mythology?"

Brother. She was smart, too. I nodded. "My father's really into space." That sounded dumb. "But not literally." I was sinking fast. "He works at Cape Kennedy." I felt like the ugly duckling next to this girl, and worse yet, a stupid ugly duckling.

Shalisa only laughed. "You must be here to apply to the school. Where did you go to school before this?"

I cleared my throat. "Uh, Astronaut Junior High."

"Where did you go to school, Shalisa?" Mom asked.

"Oh, I was at Princeton Academy this past year. My parents prefer Princeton, but my grandparents are on the board here at the Spa, and, well—" She lifted her arms dramatically and smiled. "To keep the peace, I'll go a year to each school. That way everybody's happy."

"At the Spa?" I asked, lost.

"All the old-timers call it the Spa," Shalisa explained. "School for Performing Arts—S-P-A, get it? It's a lot easier to say."

"Oh." I nodded, digesting this last bit of information. Andrea would die if I told her I was going to school at the "Spa." It sounded so snobby.

I looked again at Shalisa. No wonder she was so polished, if she had been going to school here and at Princeton, the most exclusive private school in the county. She didn't have a single rough edge: no zits, no broken nails, no accent, no bad manners, no moles, not even a freckle. She probably even had cute feet under those soft leather shoes, and Andrea always says that *nobody* has pretty feet.

I was staring at Shalisa's shoes, so my mother nudged me, not very gently, and asked Shalisa to sit down.

"Thank you, but just for a moment," Shalisa said, and then she gracefully lowered herself into the folding chair next to me. I was amazed. Most people—millions and billions of them—go into a chair rear first. Not Shalisa. She backed up so that her legs touched the edge of the chair, then she gently slid back into place. She crossed her feet delicately at the ankle, and then folded her hands in her lap.

"Well, Cassie," she said, "tell me about yourself."

She sounded like a psychiatrist. I think I was watching her with my jaw down, and I couldn't stop an abrupt "ha" from coming out of my mouth. *Andrea would love this,* I thought.

"Do you spend all your time listening to Rachmaninoff or watching PBS?" I asked. "Or do you ever just hang out?"

She blinked once, then laughed, a delicate, three-noted *ha, ha, ha.* "I'm sorry, did I give that impression?" she asked, raising a sculpted eyebrow. "I didn't mean to seem pretentious."

I made a mental note to find a dictionary and

check the meaning of *pretentious.* "It's OK," I answered, shrugging. "It's just that you seem like you're from another world. We're regular people. My mother's an interior decorator—"

"Why, that's fascinating!" She leaned over me and tapped Mom's knee. "Interior design is a demanding field. You and your daughter both must be very talented."

I had to hand it to her, nothing shook her. "I'm not so hot. But my brother's a genius."

"Really?" She looked politely surprised. "How fascinating!"

"Yeah, fascinating." I wasn't sure if I liked Shalisa or not. Talking to her was like talking to one of my mother's friends.

"What is your area of interest, Cassie?" she asked.

"Um, singing." Suddenly singing seemed plain and ordinary.

"How nice!" Shalisa smiled again. "See the girl over there in the denim skirt? That's Nancy Peavler—she's a singer, plus she plays oboe and clarinet. Timothy Jones, the boy against the door, he sings and majors in piano, percussion, and composition." She scanned the room, hoping to encourage me, no doubt, but I was feeling more and more out of place. "The girl in the far corner is Antonia DeVere. She's an actress, an artist, and a coloratura soprano. What do you sing, Cassie?"

"Anything," I mumbled. "Pop, classical, musicals."

She laughed again, *ha ha ha.* "I mean how do you classify your voice? Lyric? Coloratura? Mezzo?"

"All of them," I said, smiling. "I've very versatile."

Shalisa blinked again, confused, then flashed her smile. "Well, I hope you have good luck on the entrance auditions."

"Good luck to you, too," Mom answered, but Shalisa laughed. "Oh, I'm fairly sure I'll be here next year," she said, tossing her hair. "Children and grandchildren of board members are given priority consideration. And," she said with a playful squeeze to my arm, "I hope to have you for a classmate."

I smiled at her, but when she looked away, my smile froze, and I gave Mom my best "help" expression.

Mom just shook her head and whispered confidentially, "This was all *your* idea."

We sat like awkward bumps on a log, waiting, until three new people walked into the room. The woman was tall and thin and carried herself with an air of authority. "Mrs. Allan," Shalisa whispered, noticing my curiosity. "She's the principal of the school. The man with her is Mr. Harris, a lawyer."

The man was an ordinary, nice-looking man, but he wasn't the one who attracted my attention most. There was a boy with them, probably about fourteen or fifteen, who had dark, curly hair and an athletic build. He stood behind the

54

adults with his hands crammed into the pockets of his Princeton letter sweater, and it was obvious he was bored because he was pretending to study the floor tiles. Then he looked up, right at me.

Our eyes met, and I was so embarrassed I looked away for a second, but then I couldn't help but look back. I rolled my eyes: *I know, I'm bored too.* He actually smiled back at me for a minute before looking back down at the floor.

"Who's the kid?" I nudged Shalisa. "And why is he wearing that sweater when it's ninety-four degrees outside?"

"That's Nick Harris, Mr. Harris's son," Shalisa explained. "The sweater's part of the Princeton uniform. He'll be in the tenth grade next year, unless—" She tilted her pretty head curiously. "I wonder if he's going to enroll at the Spa?" She giggled. "I wonder if he's following *me* over here?"

"I wonder," I echoed, fiercely hoping it wasn't true.

"Thank you for coming, ladies and gentlemen." Mrs. Allan began the meeting. "The attorney for our school, Mr. Tom Harris, has just informed me that we have received permission from city council to build a new auditorium on our vacant property. Isn't that wonderful news?"

A wave of polite applause met her words, and I stole another peek at Nick Harris. He was watching Mrs. Allan, but I was surprised to see Mr. Tom Harris looking our way. He was looking at my mother.

Mrs. Allan explained that school would begin on September 4, after Labor Day, and the entrance auditions would be held during the first weekend of July. I had less than three weeks to prepare!

"The results of admissions and the scholarship grants will be announced by August 10," Mrs. Allan went on. "I'm sorry for the delay, but with vacations and so many of our families traveling abroad this summer, there's no way we can make these announcements any sooner." She smiled graciously.

The rest of the meeting centered on curriculum, the financial standing of the school, and arrangements for boarding students. Finally, after an hour, Mrs. Allan dismissed the meeting with a polite nod and an invitation for coffee and tea in an adjoining room.

Shalisa made a beeline for Nick Harris, and I stayed one step behind her the entire way. He stood quietly, with his hands in his pockets again. He was probably struck dumb by Shalisa's perfection.

"Hello, Nick, it's good to see you here," she purred. "I'd like you to meet Cassiopeia Perkins. She hopes to join us in the fall."

"Cassie," I mumbled. "My friends call me Cassie."

Nick reluctantly pulled his hand from his pocket and shook mine. I felt kind of dumb, like we were playing grown up or something. But around us, everyone was doing the same thing.

"Are you auditioning for the school, too?" I asked. "Or are you staying at Princeton?"

"Excuse me," Shalisa interrupted, glancing across the room. "There's Mrs. Johnson, my grandmother's closest friend. I've simply got to run and say hello."

She left Nick and me standing there, and I was surprised that I was a little sorry to see her go. She could be annoying, but at least she could fill a conversation.

"She's something, isn't she?" Nick asked.

I wasn't sure what he meant, but I nodded. "Yeah, she is."

"Would you like some punch?" Nick asked politely. "I could get us some."

"No, thanks," I answered, shuffling my feet awkwardly. Was I boring him? Should I leave so he could follow Shalisa? "I think I'd just like to sit down and wait for my mom."

Nick sighed in relief. "I'll join you."

We walked over to a corner of the room where chairs had been set up for people like us who didn't like to mingle.

"So are you a singer, a dancer, or what?" Nick asked as we sat down.

"A singer, or at least I hope I am," I said. "But that's all I am. Everyone else here seems to do at least three things."

"That's OK. I'm nothing artistic," Nick said,

leaning forward to watch the crowd. "I don't sing, dance, or anything. I play sports. But I think I could be a good actor."

"An actor?"

"Yeah. I've been watching my father in action for years, and I know I could act as well as he does."

"But he's a lawyer, isn't he?"

"Sure." Nick smiled at me. "Lawyers act all the time."

I laughed. He was nice, and funny, too. Better than that, it was starting to look as though he wasn't hung up on Shalisa.

"Look at my dad now," Nick said with a nod to where his dad stood talking to Mrs. Allan and, I noted with surprise, my mother. "I'll lay odds that he's charming Mrs. Allan so she'll introduce him to that lady. She's his type."

"His type? She's my mother."

"You're kidding." Nick looked at me and groaned. "I should have known. Same smile, same eyes, same hair." He shrugged. "Well, we'd better get to know one another. It's a safe bet my dad will be dating your mother."

"Are your parents divorced, too?"

"No." Nick shook his head. "My mom died when I was five."

"I'm sorry." I didn't know what else to say. "I think you're wrong about our parents, though. My mom and dad's divorce won't be final for two more months, and I don't think she's ready to date. She's into this stage where it's just her and me against the world."

"My dad went through that once," Nick said, "but as time passed he got lonesome, I guess. Now he dates a lot. But that's it, he just dates. We've got Uncle Jacob to run things at the house."

"Uncle Jacob?"

"Jacob Benton. Haven't you seen his column in the newspaper?"

I shook my head. I didn't read the paper very often.

"Uncle Jacob lives with us and runs things—hires the maid and the cook, and keeps me company when Dad's out of town. He works at home, so it works out well for all of us."

"Your uncle's a writer?" I thought of all the silly and serious poems in my private notebook at home. I had always wondered what a real writer would think of them.

"Yeah." He leaned his chair back and put an arm around my chair to steady himself. "So what about you? Got a boyfriend or something?"

"Or something." I smiled, thinking of Chip. "There's a guy at my old school, but it's nothing serious. We're just good friends."

"OK." Mr. Harris was motioning in our direction, so Nick stood up to leave. "Then I hope I see you again sometime."

"Me, too." The words popped out of my mouth before I even knew what I was saying.

7

"So, what did you think?" Mom asked as we drove home.

"I don't know." I looked at the stately homes as we drove away from the school, homes that seemed to represent the class and elegance everyone at the Spa had—everyone except me. "I don't know if I have what it takes. There were *lots* of singers, and most of them didn't just sing. They all either played an instrument or danced or composed symphonies or something."

"Are you saying you want to back out?" Mom's voice was gentle. "We haven't mailed in the application forms, you know. We could just forget the whole thing."

I shrugged. "I guess I should think about it a while."

When we got home, I went into my room, stretched out across the bed, and pulled out my private notebook. Across the top of the first empty page I wrote "Shalisa McRay." Across the second page I scrawled "Cassie Perkins." As best I could, which wasn't very well, I drew Shalisa's big eyes, her pretty hair, and her figure under her name. I couldn't help but laugh. A three year old could draw better, so I gave up and just drew a stick figure on my page. On each page, I made a list:

Shalisa McRay	Cassie Perkins
beautiful	ordinary
rich	divorce-poor
knows important people	knows ordinary people
from private school	from public school
can probably do everything	can sing and write poetry
polished	klutzy
smart	ordinary
pretty feet	ugly toes
Conclusion: can't fail to get into Spa	Conclusion: probably can't get in

It didn't take long to realize I was doomed. Those people at that meeting were from a different planet, where everyone could chitchat and

62

wear cardigan sweaters in June without sweating. Planet Snobula. I'd never fit in. The only halfway ordinary person there was Nick, but his father was the school's lawyer, and if he wanted to go to school at the Spa, it would somehow be arranged. Nobody was going to pull any strings for me. My father sure wouldn't, and my mother couldn't.

If my competition were people like Shalisa and Nick, I wouldn't have a chance even if I sang like Whitney Houston. "I'm going to forget it," I whispered to Suki. "It'll be a waste of time and effort."

The phone rang, and I let Mom answer it. A few seconds later she knocked on my door. "It's for you," she said, a mischievous smile on her face. "It's a boy."

Uh oh. I picked up my extension and squeaked, "Hello?"

"How was the meeting?" It was Chip. "Are you a star yet?"

"No way," I answered, burrowing my head into my pillow and holding the phone against my ear. "I don't think it's going to work out."

"Why not?"

"I don't know." How could I make Chip understand? "Everyone there is *so* talented. Most kids play three or four instruments, and I don't do anything except sing, and I've never had voice lessons or anything."

"Cassie, so where do you think you'll learn?

They don't expect you to come in knowing everything. They're looking for potential!"

"I don't know, Chip." I felt a sob rising in my throat, and I had to be quiet until the feeling passed.

"Are you OK, Cassie?"

Like a dummy, I nodded.

"Cassie? Are you upset?"

I nodded again, but this time I managed to squeak out, "Uh huh."

"Don't let it get you down." Chip's voice was firm and almost stern. "You wanted to try to do this, right?"

"Uh huh."

"Remember how badly you wanted the part in *Oklahoma?* Well, make yourself want this just as badly. Give it your best shot. That's all you can do, but you'll be sorry if you back out now."

I took a deep breath to calm myself and thought about last year when I went out for the part in junior high. "It was different with *Oklahoma!*" I said. "No one knew I could sing, except Max, and I auditioned on my own. If I hadn't gotten the part, no one would have known. But if I show up at Astronaut High next year, everyone will know I blew it, unless I tell them I changed my mind."

"They won't see it like that," Chip said. "They'll just think you took a chance at doing something you really wanted to do. That takes guts, Cassie."

"Well, I don't feel very gutsy right now," I

snapped. I knew I was being rude, especially since Chip was trying to help, but I didn't want to hear a pep talk. "I'm really tired, Chip, and I ought to go."

"OK. But I called to see if you wanted to meet me at the mall tomorrow night. We could catch a movie and then get some ice cream or something." He sounded proud and confident. "I've got my first paycheck, and I'd like to take you out."

"Um, I'll have to ask my mom." Was this a date or what? Any other girl at my school would have killed to go out with Chip, but I wasn't sure I wanted to encourage anything more than a friendship. Still it would be fun to go out with him, and it'd take my mind off the Spa.

"I don't think she'll let me go alone, Chip, so can Andrea come along?"

"Sure." Chip even sounded a little relieved. "I'll meet you at the mall's theater entrance at seven o'clock, OK?"

"OK." Maybe this summer wouldn't be so bad after all.

Mom had left the application forms out on the kitchen counter, so they were the first thing I saw the next morning. Staring at them, I lost both my appetite for breakfast and the nice feeling I'd had since Chip called.

"What are those?" Max startled me. He was at the kitchen bar reading the newspaper.

"When did you get here?"

"Dad dropped me off last night after you went

to bed. I'm here all week, remember?" He winked at me. "Lucky you."

"Right." I had forgotten that Max was coming for two whole weeks instead of just the weekend because he and Dad were going on a six-week trip in July and August.

"So what's with the papers?" Max asked again.

"They're application forms for the Spa."

"Spa?" Max thought a moment. "School for Performing Arts, right?"

"Bingo, boy genius."

"So why were you standing here making faces at the forms?" He stood up on his stool and reached for the cupboard where Mom kept his Twinkies. "And will you hand me the milk, please?"

While Max settled in with his favorite breakfast of Twinkies dunked in milk, I explained about the school and how inferior I felt at the meeting.

"Maybe you were just overwhelmed," Max suggested. "I'll bet one on one you could take anybody there."

"No." I shook my head. "There's this girl named Shalisa who looks like Christie Brinkley and acts like Miss National Congeniality."

"What's her talent?" Max asked, his mouth full.

I stopped to think. "That's funny. I don't think she ever said."

"See there?" Max pointed the end of a soggy Twinkie in my direction. "Maybe you've got more talent in your little finger than she has in her whole body, but you were just over-whelmed. You should give the Spa a chance. *You* could overwhelm *them*."

Max had always been clear-headed, and he convinced me. "I'll do it," I said, picking up the forms and looking for a pencil. "I'll get these in the mail today, choose a song for the audition, and call Mr. Williams to help coach me. The audition's on July 7, so it's not like I'll be wasting my entire summer on it."

Max looked up and smiled, a milk moustache circling his lips. He looked so adorable I could have kissed him.

8

I had just come back from putting my application in the mailbox when the phone rang.
Mom answered it as I muttered under my breath:
"Please, Chip, don't break off our plans for tonight!"

But it wasn't Chip. The call was for Mom.
"Why, Mr. Harris," I heard her say, and then,
"Of course, Tom. That would be lovely."

I stationed myself in the hall to listen. Max
came out of his room and saw me, so I put my
finger over my lips.

"Tonight?" Mom said. "No, we didn't have
any plans. Nothing that we couldn't change,
anyway."

How could she forget about me? I was
instantly furious, but then she remembered.

"Oh, Tom, there's a small problem. Cassie's
meeting some of her school friends at the mall

at seven o'clock." She laughed. "I don't think she'd forgive me if she couldn't go. You know how kids are."

She listened for a minute, then said, "That would work beautifully." She was using the smooth voice she used with her decorating clients. "We'll just drop them all at the mall and pick them up later. Fine. See you then."

She came around the corner, humming a little tune, and caught Max and me standing in the hall. She raised an eyebrow but kept walking. "Yes, you heard correctly," she called over her shoulder. "Mr. Harris is taking us all to dinner tonight at the Black Swan. You can go to the movie afterward. Max, wear your coat and tie if you have one here. Cassie, why don't you wear your red dress? It's so pretty."

She stopped outside her bedroom and gave us a dazzling smile. "So let's get busy and do whatever we have to do, OK? He'll pick us up at five-thirty, and I've got to get ready."

Max and I watched in amazement as our mother started to get ready for a date seven and a half hours early.

Not knowing what else to do, I called Andrea. "It's horrible," I wailed into the phone. "Mom and Mr. Harris are dropping *all* of us at the mall."

"It's really not that bad, Cassie," Andrea assured me. "Since your date's with Chip, let me sit with Nick. Max can just pal around with us. He's not a problem."

I didn't want to come out and tell her, but I'd

70

always considered Chip more of a friend. It was *Nick* I was thinking of as a potential boyfriend—*my* potential boyfriend.

"Why don't we sit Max, then you, then Chip, then me, and then Nick?" I suggested. "Since you know Chip already, he will be more comfortable talking to you."

Andrea was smooth. "Max won't want to sit next to dumb ol' me," she said. "Why don't we sit Max, then you, then Nick, then me, and then Chip?"

Sure, I thought. *Put yourself between two guys and me next to my brother!*

"Why don't we just wait until we get there," I suggested. "What happens, happens."

I hadn't seen my mother this excited in months, if not years. She took a long, hot bath, shaved her legs, styled her hair, and walked around in her bathrobe for hours. "I only wish I had time to lose ten pounds," she said, watching Max and me eat a snack. "I don't have a thing to wear."

That was an exaggeration, of course, and at four o'clock five different outfits were laid out on the bed. I sat on the edge of her bed and watched her put on her makeup. "So you're going out on a date, huh?" I asked, trying to make small talk. "I really didn't think you wanted to date anybody."

"I know it sounds silly to you kids," she said, putting on a double coat of mascara, "but you've got to understand that on any given day the only adult conversation I have is either with my stubborn clients or telephone salesmen. I'm looking forward to the company. Tom seems very nice, and so does his son. You don't mind having him join you and your friends tonight, do you?"

I shrugged, not knowing how to explain it. I'd have loved to be with Nick any other time, but it was going to be a little awkward with Chip, Andrea, and Max there, too.

"Actually, honey," Mom went on, stretching her lips to apply her lip liner, "I'm glad you came in. We need to have a little talk about dating. You're going into the ninth grade, and I know this is the time when boys start to notice girls and girls start to notice boys."

She wasn't looking at me, so I rolled my eyes. We girls had been noticing boys for years.

"Anyway, you're too young to begin formal dating, but I don't mind you going to the mall with your friends, even if some of them are boys." She caught my eye in the mirror and winked. "But we need to set a few ground rules. First, you should know that it's very dangerous to wander away from the group. If you go to the mall with your friends, I want you to stay with your friends."

"OK." I thought she was overreacting with this speech, but I didn't want to start a fight. I'd been to the mall with my friends zillions of times. But it had always been Dad or Andrea's mom who dropped us off.

"And I don't want you to ever lie to me. If you say you're going to be at the mall, I expect you to be at the mall. If you show me now that I can trust you, then when you're older you'll have more freedom. But if you show me that I *can't* trust you, well, you'll have less freedom when you want it most. Understand?"

I nodded at her reflection, and she seemed satisfied. She picked up her blush brush and dabbed at her cheekbones. "One more thing—I hope you know what proper behavior is. If you're in doubt, just ask yourself, 'Would people think less of me if they saw me now?' That's a good guideline. Do you understand, Cassie?"

I nodded again, hoping she was finished. Honestly, she could be so out of it sometimes. I knew Andrea would have said that speech was "like, antiquated." But Mom turned from the mirror and patted my leg. "Honey, I'm not sure I can handle parenting alone with you dating and all. But if you'll work with me, I think we can get through it OK. I'm glad we had this talk."

I murmured, "Me, too," and left her room. Back in my own room, I fell on my bed and sighed. Was that our big dating talk? I laughed, wondering if I should give one to my mom now that she was dating again. My dad had been dating for a while, so I figured it was natural for Mom, too. But it still felt strange.

I rolled over onto my stomach and hugged my pillow. What a mess. My parents were almost divorced and already dating other people; I was about to go out on my first date with two boys, my best friend, and my little brother. Life could sure get complicated.

The Black Swan restaurant was uncomfortable. The carpet was black and thick, and a corps of black-coated waiters stood by every table to jump to every little gesture. Mr. Harris asked me and Max what we liked to eat, and then he ordered for the entire table, the fancy French tripping elegantly off of his tongue.

My dad would have never taken us to a place like that. To him, food wasn't food unless it had pasta, oregano, or tomato sauce in it or on it.

Nick looked different tonight, sort of stiff and uncomfortable. I liked him better in his jeans and sweater with his hands in his pockets. Max was sulky, too, and kept twisting his neck because his tie was uncomfortable. We three kids sat awkwardly on our side of the table while Mom and Mr. Harris talked and laughed.

The most embarrassing thing happened when I reached for my dinner roll and cracked it open. It was a hard dinner roll, and as I broke it, a few crumbs fell onto the black table cloth. It was no big deal, but the Black Swan Guys were determined to make it the highlight of the evening.

"One minute, mademoiselle," a waiter murmured, and suddenly there was a waiter at each of my elbows. One scraped the crumbs off the table with a little scraper gadget, and the other held a delicate china dish at the edge of the table for the crumbs to fall into. I almost expected a guy with a trumpet to come out and blow while someone else announced: "Cassie Perkins has just crumbed our table!"

When the crumb crew had left, I leaned over and whispered to Max: "Don't touch the roll. And whatever you do, don't spill anything."

From the corner of my eye, I could see Nick smile. "Don't worry about it," he said quietly. "Sometimes I spill things just to see them scramble."

Max snickered and our parents looked up in surprise. "What's so funny?" Mom asked.

"Nothing much," I answered. "We're just having a good time."

After dinner Mr. Harris drove us to the mall in his Mercedes. Chip and Andrea were sitting on a bench by the theater entrance, right on time, and I guessed Andrea had explained things to Chip, because he didn't look happy. Andrea, though, looked very hopeful.

"Remember, we'll pick you up here right at nine-thirty," Mom told us. "And don't be late or I'll call the police to look for you."

"Is she kidding?" Nick asked as we slid out of the car.

"No, she's not," I answered. "She's a mother."

We walked toward Chip and Andrea. "Chip, Andrea, this is Nick," I introduced them. "His dad took us all out to dinner, so Nick is joining us now."

Andrea looked at Nick and then winked and smiled at me.

"My dad wanted to treat all of us," Nick said, pulling out his wallet. "He gave me plenty of money."

"That's OK, I wanted to pay for—," Chip began, but I put my hand on his arm to interrupt him.

"That's OK, Chip. Mr. Harris wanted to do it." I felt as though I were walking on a high wire: I wanted Nick to think Chip was just a friend, which he was, but I didn't want Chip to get upset about Nick, either.

"We'd better get inside," Max spoke up. "The movie starts in five minutes, and I don't have my popcorn yet."

Max and the guys moved toward the ticket window, but Andrea hung back and grabbed my arm. "So, who gets who?" she asked.

I shook her hand off; I was too tired for games. "I don't know," I said with a shrug. "But come on. It's going to be interesting."

The seating inside was a disaster. For once, the guys remembered "ladies first" and hung back long enough for Andrea to head down the row. She was hoping that Chip or Nick would follow, but Max did, happily munching on his popcorn with extra butter. Chip followed Max, resentfully, and Nick, like a good host, waited outside in the aisle for me to file in. So there I was, with Chip on my left and Nick on my right, while Andrea was stuck down on the end with Max. *She'll kill me tomorrow,* I thought.

I wasn't enjoying myself. I knew Chip was hurt for two reasons: first, this was supposed to be our date, and now Nick had come along and taken charge of everything. Second, Chip had been really proud of earning his own money, and Nick had come along and *bought* everything. Once Chip leaned over to me and said, "Cassie, can I get you anything? Junior Mints? A candy bar? Sweet Tarts?" but my hands were full of the jumbo popcorn and the giant Coke Nick had bought me. I shook my head.

Nick was leaning his arm and shoulder on the armrest we shared on my right, and Chip was doing the same thing on my left. I sat stiffly, my arms tightly to my sides, careful not to lean either way. After two hours, my neck was stiff and my arms ached.

We filed out of the movie, and Chip tried to smile and take charge. "How about ice cream?" he smiled, looking at me. "I'll treat everybody."

"It's 9:15," Nick pointed out. "I'd hate to have Cassie's mom call the police if I don't have her back in time."

Chip spoke directly to me. "Cassie? Ice cream?"

I wanted to, and I would have if I could have, but I had to shake my head. "I'm sorry, Chip, but I'm stuffed. I ate a whole jumbo popcorn."

Chip looked over to where Andrea sat sulking on a bench. "Andrea? Ice cream?"

I felt a strange twinge of jealousy. Andrea

answered in a voice dripping with sarcasm: "Me? You mean someone other than Max wants to be with me?"

"Come on, Andrea." Chip pulled her up by the hand. "What's your favorite flavor? Mint chip? Rocky Road?"

Andrea laughed then, and as they walked away from us I could hear her laughter echoing down the nearly deserted mall. "Let's go," I said, feeling a little sick. "I don't feel so good."

"Probably all that popcorn on top of the Black Swan," Nick said, leading the way out. "I'm glad we'll be back early. My dad says I should always be back early to impress the girl's parents, um, I mean, parent."

Mr. Harris's Mercedes pulled up precisely two minutes early. Was that to impress us? Nick opened the door, and Max and I slid into the back. "Hi," Nick said, sliding in beside us. "I hope you two had as much fun as we did."

Max looked at me, and I gave him a sick little smile.

9

"Well, how was your first date?" Mom asked, sinking onto my bed. How could she call it that? I wondered. It wasn't a date, it was a circus. I didn't think anybody but Max had had a good time.

But it was obvious Mom wouldn't understand. The whole mess had been her fault, anyway, because she invited Nick and Max to go along.

"It was OK," I answered, staring at the ceiling. "A little crowded."

A frown wrinkled Mom's forehead. "Crowded? I thought it would work out perfectly. Didn't Andrea like Nick?"

I sighed. Wasn't anyone going to give *me* a chance at Nick?

"She liked him fine, I guess. But she ended up at the ice cream parlor with Chip."

Mom nodded. "I see," she said, standing up.

"Well, get a good sleep now. See you in the morning."

She stopped by the doorway, though, and turned out the light. As she looked toward me in the dim light from the hallway, I could see her smile. "Aren't you a little curious to know how *my* date went?"

No, I wasn't. But I knew she was dying to tell me, so I mumbled, "How was it?"

She actually giggled. "Great. It was great. Tom is a wonderful man. I think you'd really like him, Cassie, and Max would, too."

I faked a yawn. "That's nice, Mom."

She took the hint and left. I turned toward the wall and sighed. From her place at the foot of my bed, Suki began to snore. I began to cry. If my parents hadn't split up, none of this would be happening. It was all their fault.

The next morning I decided to put my love life on a shelf, at least temporarily, and concentrate on my audition for the Spa. "Everyone around here can just jump in a lake for all I care," I muttered to myself as I pulled down our thick telephone book. "If no one around here wants to help me, at least I know someone who will." Fortunately, the number I wanted was listed.

The phone rang and a lady answered in a sleepy voice. "Hello?"

"Hello, I'm trying to reach Mr. James Williams, the choir teacher at Astronaut Junior High."

She laughed softly. "School's out, honey."

I sighed. "Is he there, please?"

"Just a minute. I'll have to go get him. I think he's outside mowing the lawn."

I glanced at the clock. Brother. Eight-thirty on a Saturday morning probably wasn't the best time to call. I had probably got Mrs. Williams out of bed, not to mention bringing Mr. Williams in from mowing his lawn.

It was funny, but I'd never thought about Mr. Williams having a lawn before, with a house, a wife, and kids. Maybe he even had a dog. I tried to picture him at home, with his dog bringing him his slippers and his wife handing him the newspaper. Or vice versa. But the image just wouldn't come. It was easier to picture him living at his desk at school and sleeping in a practice room.

"Hello?"

"Mr. Williams?"

"Yes, who is this?" He sounded mildly aggravated, and I was a little scared. What if he hadn't meant what he said when he volunteered to help me?

"It's Cassie Perkins. I'm going to audition for the School for Performing Arts in a couple of weeks, and I wondered if you still wanted to help coach me."

"Oh yes, Cassie." It was good to hear that he remembered, but I was still a little concerned. He wasn't exactly jumping for joy that I'd called. "What did you have in mind?"

I was stunned. I didn't have *anything* in mind, I thought he would take care of all that. "I don't know," I answered.

"Well, what have you prepared?"

"Nothing."

"I see." I could just see him standing at his kitchen telephone, hot and sweaty, thinking that Cassie Perkins was the dumbest, most ill-prepared, presumptuous girl he had ever known. He had been my only hope, and I could feel my dream come crashing down under a wave of guilt and embarrassment.

"I'm sorry, Mr. Williams," I blurted out. "I don't have to do this. I don't want to impose, and it's a bad idea. I'm sorry I bothered you and woke up your wife or whatever. Good-bye—"

"Wait, Cassie. Do you have any plans for this afternoon?"

"No, sir."

"OK. I think I can find a couple of hours and some music around here that might do. Can you find someone to bring you over?"

"Sure."

He said he'd see me at two, and he hung up. I breathed a sigh of relief. At least someone hadn't let me down.

Mr. Williams lived in a little blue and white house with a wide lawn. When I rang the door-bell, a white-haired woman answered and smiled at me. "You must be Cassie. Come on in, honey."

I recognized her voice; she sounded sleepy

even now. She led me into the living room, where Mr. Williams was sitting at the piano, surrounded by piles of music books. "Good to see you, Cassie," he said, smiling. "I see you've met my mother."

Oops. The woman wasn't his wife; she was his mother. "Nice to meet you," I said, feeling my cheeks redden.

"Nice to meet you, too," she called over her shoulder as she padded through the living room in her slippers. "If you need anything, you just holler."

Mr. Williams played a quick chord on the piano. "How's the voice? No trouble?"

I shook my head. "I don't think so."

He nodded. "Good. I've found two pieces of music, each very different from the other, but suitable for you. You can learn them both and then perform the one with which you feel most comfortable. Then if you need an encore piece, you'll have something ready."

I nodded, and he pulled a sheet of music from the top of the piano. "This is 'I Enjoy Being a Girl,'" he said, pointing to the lyric. "It's a show tune, lots of fun, and a little flirty. You can stage it if you like. Maybe Andrea can teach you a few little steps to keep it interesting."

He pulled out a thick book and opened to a different song. "'Villanelle' is more difficult," he said, pointing thoughtfully to the open page. "It's very light, very high, and contains coloratura passages that are very fast. To sing it, your voice must be like a flute, just flitting over the high notes as delicately as a piccolo. It's a lot to ask from a girl your age, but I think your voice could handle it if you work hard. Do you think you'd like to try?"

I nodded. I'd heard that word *coloratura* from Shalisa, and I wanted to do it. Besides, the competition would demand that I do something especially outstanding. Simply singing a popular song wouldn't cut it.

Mr. Williams smiled. "Good. There's just one more thing." He hesitated a moment. "I know I said I'd coach you, and I will. But I'm afraid my time is limited. I'll work with you today, and perhaps one other time, but Cassie, I'm getting married next month, and I'm afraid I can't do any more."

I was amazed. Andrea and Chip would be flabbergasted. "Uh, congratulations," I said. "That's great."

Mr. Williams turned to the piano. "Thanks. Now, shall we get started?" We worked hard for two hours, then Mr. Williams said he had to stop. He had a date.

I walked home, humming snatches of "I Enjoy Being a Girl" and trying to visualize how it could be performed. It was a cute song, and maybe I could even come up with some kind of outfit to dress up my performance. It simply had to be incredibly good to get me into the school and win me a scholarship.

I didn't even want to think about singing

"Villanelle." It was a pretty song, as far as art songs go, but it was hard to sing, plus it didn't have a meaningful or cute or romantic message. It was about songster swallows flying swiftly— hard enough to *say,* much less *sing.* But Mr. Williams said art songs were designed to show off technique and artistry, so I promised him I'd work on it. However, I was going to count on "I Enjoy Being a Girl."

As I walked home, I couldn't help but think about the secret life of Mr. Williams. I guess it wasn't a secret to his family, his neighbors, or anyone who really knew him. But I had been in his classroom after school every day for nearly three months, and I had had no idea he had a girlfriend, let alone was engaged. Maybe it was shocking and disappointing because somehow I'd believed that Mr. Williams was someone I could count on, someone who cared about me. But when it came to real life, I had to admit I didn't even know the man.

10

When I got home, Max was in the kitchen dressed in his lab coat and plastic goggles. "Is that your scientist outfit?" I asked. "Or are you a welder today?"

Max ignored my teasing and nodded seriously without taking his eyes off a beaker full of green goop he was holding up to the light. "My experiment," he said. "I'm a scientist."

I pulled a stool up to the kitchen bar and looked over at his mess. "Is that the algae you were growing? Did Mom actually let you bring that stuff from Dad's?"

"I explained to her that I was on the verge of a propitious breakthrough," Max explained, "and since I'm here all week, she agreed to let me bring everything. Of course, it only took a little dropperful of the algae," he said, stirring the goop in the beaker with a glass rod. "This stuff grows like wildfire if the conditions are right."

"You're on the verge, huh?" I said, pulling my music books to me and starting for my room. "Sounds great."

"Want to hear about it?" Max called, pulling his goggles to the top of his head. "I think this idea could actually be commercially successful."

I had other things on my mind. "Later, Max," I called.

Later on, Nick called. "Boy, is this ever a day for surprises," I told him. "First I hear Mr. Williams is getting married, and now you."

"I'm getting married?" Nick laughed.

"No, silly, it's just that I didn't expect you to call." The pressure of having Chip and Andrea around was gone, and I found that talking to Nick was as easy as it had been at the school.

"I'm sorry if I barged in at the movie," he said. "I felt bad because Dad just kind of invited me along with you and your friends."

"Don't feel bad," I assured him. "I was glad you could come." Which was true, I reminded myself. I just wish it had been another time and place.

"Are you auditioning for the Spa?" I asked him. "I worked on my music all afternoon."

"No. I've decided to go back to Princeton and stay in sports. Dad doesn't care where I go, as long as it's a good private school so I can get into an Ivy League college."

I told him he was lucky he didn't have to worry about the auditions.

"You'll do fine," he told me. "You're one in a million."

I felt a glow rise from my toes to my cheeks, and I was glad he couldn't see me. "Thanks," I answered. "But you've never even heard me sing."

"I don't have to," he said. "I know you'll be great."

Just then my mom walked by. "Is that Nick?" she whispered. "And are you almost done?"

I nodded, and she practically grabbed the phone from me. "Nick, is your father available?" she asked. Nick must have gone to get his dad, because Mom held the phone away for a minute while she looked in my mirror and smoothed her hair.

"Hello, Tom?" She straightened up. "It's Claire. Listen, since you were kind enough to treat us to dinner last night, why don't I cook dinner for you next weekend?"

She giggled like a little kid and I watched her, amazed. "Well, Cassie and Max will be at their father's place, so it will be just the two of us, if that's OK."

She murmured and laughed softly for a few minutes more, then said softly, "OK. Seven on Saturday. See you then." She hung up the phone without even asking me if I was done talking to Nick.

"He's coming here for dinner next Saturday?"
I asked.

She nodded. "Yes."

"What about Nick?" I was a little upset that
my mother had ignored my own budding
romance, as trivial as it may have seemed to her.
"Aren't you going to feed Nick, too? Why don't
I skip my weekend with Dad so Nick can come,
and I'll be here, and—"

"No," she said abruptly, cutting me off. "No
kids. Besides, it's your weekend with your father,
and he'll be counting on you."

Something wasn't quite right. "But what
about the dating rule?" I asked.

"What dating rule?"

"The one about 'what will other people
think?' Mom, if we're gone and you have a man
over here, people will think, well, terrible
things."

She turned and looked at me as if she'd never
seen me before. "Cassie Perkins, I can't believe
what I'm hearing," she said slowly. "You're
thirteen years old, and you're trying to tell me
how to conduct myself."

"I'm nearly fourteen," I answered, a little
insulted. "And I don't see why dating for you
should be any different than dating for me. I
mean, you can go where you want when you
want, but if the main thing is what people will
think, why don't you care about that? You're
still married to my father, you know. The
divorce isn't final."

I thought she'd scream at me, but she didn't. "Why are you doing this?" She sat on the end of my bed and calmly crossed her legs. "Honey, I know it may seem strange for you to think of another man being here in this house, especially since your father has left. And it is probably strange that I'm dating at all. As for the divorce, well, your father has made it perfectly clear that our marriage is over, no matter what the court says about when the divorce is official. I'm an adult, Cass, and you're just going to have to trust me."

Mom got up to leave, and a reckless thought popped into my head. Before I knew it, the words had flown out of my mouth: "Do you trust me?"

Mom leaned against my door and looked at me. Her face was red, and I knew now she was dangerously close to being very angry. "Yes, I trust you. Is there any reason why I shouldn't?"

"If I was alone in the house with Nick, would you trust me?"

"You won't be alone in the house with any boy, young lady," she said, straightening up. "I forbid it. It's my house."

"Why not, if you trust me?"

"Because you're young, and young people don't always have self-control. You don't know the hazards of everything, and you might be so in love with experience and emotion that you might lose your good sense. Besides—"

She paused, waving her hands uselessly. "It just looks bad."

"Yeah?" I rose up to my knees on my bed. "Well, I think it looks bad for people in the neighborhood to see a strange man entering my father's house with you alone. Max and I won't be here, and I just don't like it."

I had never, ever spoken to my mother like that before, and I thought that any minute she'd slap me. But Mom's temper suddenly cooled, and she looked at me with a half smile on her face. "Is this all an attempt to get me to invite Nick and let you stay home?" she asked. "Is that it? You've got a crush on Nick?"

I wished it were that simple, but it was more than that. I shook my head. How could I explain that I just didn't want another man sitting in my father's house, in his chair, and eating off his plate? Mr. Tom Harris was not my father, and he never would be. But I couldn't say those things to Mom. My father had walked out of here voluntarily. It wasn't all her fault.

I sank back onto my bed. "Never mind," I mumbled.

"OK," Mom answered, turning to leave. "But if it makes you feel any better about the neighbors, I'll leave all the curtains open when Tom's here."

11

The week practically flew by. Mom, Max, and I were living in the same house like we did before the divorce, but now we were all in our own worlds. I spent almost all my time working on my songs. Max was busy, too, working on his experiment in the kitchen, so Mom and I just stayed out of his way as much as we could. Neither of us wanted algae in our food.

Mom walked around the house humming happily. Tom Harris's law firm hired her to redecorate their office, so she was out of the house with her swatch books and wallpaper samples every afternoon. She wasn't griping about money anymore, and she even called her aerobics teacher and signed back up for the lessons she had canceled. There was a new spring to her step that I liked, but the happy humming was about to drive me insane.

For once I was glad that we had a piano and that I knew how to play it. Mom and Dad had bought the piano when I was in third grade. I took lessons for a year, but after that I lost interest and the piano collected dust. But now that I couldn't run to school and practice every day with Mr. Williams, I had to practice alone. I was just good enough to pick out my part on the piano, even though it was with only one finger.

"I Enjoy Being a Girl" was a fun song. The words were easy to learn, and by the end of the week I had it memorized. That was good because it was time to add motions and a few movements and to plan my costume. The song talked about a frilly dress, so I planned to borrow my mom's lace blouse and wear a skirt to match. It would be fun!

I worked on "Villanelle" at first just because Mr. Williams asked me to. It was just a dumb song about birds, but more than that, it was hard. There were little trills and frills in the melody, plus the melody jumped all around from note to note, and I was having a hard time following the music. Worst of all, there was a passage where I did nothing but sing "ah" up and down a scale, fast, and then I was supposed to jump up to a high C and then down again. Mr. Williams was right; I felt more like a piccolo than a singer.

Max peeked into the living room once while I was practicing "Villanelle." "You sound like you're laughing," he said. "Shouldn't you sound more like a tube of toothpaste?"

"Toothpaste?" I swiveled around on the piano bench. "What do you know about it?"

"Not much," he shrugged. "But the other day on PBS a lady was singing a song like that, and she said she pictured herself as a tube of toothpaste, stretching the notes out without any breaks."

"No breaks?" I still didn't understand.

"You're singing ha-ha-ha-ha-ha," Max pointed out. "It should be a continuous sound."

He was right. I looked closer at the music, and all the scale passages were marked with slurs. The jumpy places were marked with staccato notes—those were supposed to be jumpy ha-has.

I opened my mouth and tried to think like toothpaste. "Ah-ah-ah-ah-ah-ah, ah, ah," I sang up the scale.

Max nodded. "That's better. You'll be an opera singer if you keep it up."

"Right." I leaned over my music and pencilled in "toothpaste" at the top of the page. Who had time to dream about being an opera singer? All I wanted to do was get through one audition.

The doorbell rang, and Max answered it as I kept singing. "Ah-ah-ah-ah-ah—"

"Who are you, Snow White?" Andrea peeked in at me. "What are you doing? I could hear you from the street."

"I'm learning a song for the audition," I explained. "It's very dumb and very hard."

Andrea crinkled her nose. "Ugh, how can you stand to sit in the house on a day like today? Come on, let's go lie out in the sun. Or you can come to my house and we'll swim—the pool's great. Come on, Cassie. Lighten up."

I shook my head. "I can't. The audition will be here soon, and I'm not ready. But I'm glad you're here." I picked up my copy of "I Enjoy Being a Girl" and passed it to Andrea. "Can you help me stage this song? It's really cute."

Andrea skimmed through the words and laughed. "You're singing this? Can't you do something more up to date?"

"No." I felt defensive. "It's a Rodgers and Hammerstein song from the Broadway play *Flower Drum Song,* and it's cute when you hear it. Besides, it's all I've got. So can you help me stage it?"

Andrea nodded. "OK, in a minute. But first I want to talk to you about Chip."

I sighed. "What about Chip? Did you enjoy your ice cream the other night?"

"Cut it out, Cassie. I'm the one who ought to be upset about the other night. I can't believe you sat between both guys and left me on the end with Max!"

I turned around to face her and pulled my knees up to my chest on the piano bench. "It wasn't fun for me, I promise. I was miserable."

She snorted. "I would love to be that miserable. But I'm not mad anymore, I just want to know how you feel."

There was something stirring in Andrea's eyes, but I couldn't tell what she was getting at. "About what?"

"I mean, do you like Chip or Nick?"

I hesitated. "I've always liked Chip as a friend," I said. "*You* were the one who had the crush on him last year. To me he's always been just a good friend."

"And Nick?"

I smiled and looked down at my toes. "I don't know. I guess I'd like to have him as a boyfriend, but I don't know for sure how he feels about me." I couldn't help feeling a little insecure. "Don't you think he's cute?"

"Yeah, he's cute. So if you like Nick, you won't mind if—"

"What?"

"Well, you won't mind if Chip goes out with me?"

I couldn't believe what I was hearing. My best girlfriend wanted to go with my best boyfriend? I pretended not to care, but that strange jealousy nibbled at my stomach again. I shrugged. "Hey, if you guys like each other, fine."

"Good." Andrea breathed a sigh of relief and tossed her blonde hair confidently. "Because he's been calling me, and I didn't want you to find out and be upset."

I turned back to the piano. "I wouldn't be upset," I said, opening my music, "but if you don't mind, I really need to learn this song, OK? I'll see you later."

I played a chord, and Andrea stood up stiffly. "OK," she said, uncertainly. "I guess I'll see you."

I nodded. "Sure."

Mom came in, huffing and puffing. "Whew, it's got to be at least ninety-eight degrees out there today," she said, throwing a stack of mail down on the kitchen counter. She peered at Max's experiment. "Any closer today, honey?"

"I think so," Max answered. "I think I'll be done before Dad and I go on our trip."

"That's right," Mom said, nodding. "I almost forgot. How's the music coming, Cassie?"

I was sitting at the kitchen counter drinking a glass of lemonade, and I took a sip and answered her. "Fine, except that it makes me thirsty. It's hard work."

"I know it is," Mom replied, sitting down on the stool next to me. "Max, honey, can you pour your mother a glass of lemonade, too? I'm parched."

"I'll get it," I said, getting up. I knew Max was busy with his experiment, so I filled a glass with ice and pulled the lemonade pitcher out of the refrigerator. I poured her a glassful and even put a straw in it, just for pizzazz.

"Your father used to sing until he'd lose his voice," Mom said, quietly remembering. She smiled. "He'd sing that silly old song to you when you were little—what was it?"

"'My Wild Irish Rose,'" I answered. "I can still hear him singing it." An idea struck me. "Mom,

98

why didn't Dad ever sing in public? He was good enough, wasn't he?"

Mom sipped her lemonade and nodded. "Yes, he was very good, but he just never wanted to sing in front of anyone but us. I always thought he was shy."

"Dad is *not* shy," Max interrupted.

"No, I guess not." Mom stirred the ice in her glass with her straw. "I don't know why he never sang in public. But he always sang around the house. When we were first married, he'd sing 'Up-Up and Away' to me because that was his dream—flying. He wanted to work for NASA more than anything else in the world."

"'Up-Up and Away'?" I crinkled my nose. "I don't know that one."

Mom laughed. "The year we met, it was a big hit by the Fifth Dimension. He was a senior in college, and I had just graduated from high school." She took a sip from her straw and began to sing softly, "Up-up and away in my beautiful, my beautiful balloon. . . ."

"How romantic." My voice was sarcastic, and it snapped Mom out of her mood.

"You had to be there," she said. Her eyes fell on the pile of mail, and she began sorting it into three piles: hers, Dad's, and junk. "Max, be sure to take your father's mail to him this weekend, OK? I'll just stick it in your room."

"Better put it in his briefcase," I called as she walked by. "That way you know he won't forget it."

"Good idea," Mom answered, and she began singing softly. Only this time it wasn't "Up-Up and Away." It was "The Next Time I Fall in Love."

12

Dad picked us up on Friday afternoon, and as I got into the car I realized I had never made it over to Andrea's house. It was my fault, of course, and I'd have to stage my song without her expert help. But that was OK. For some reason I didn't want to be around Andrea if Chip called. All along I had thought that Chip and I were really good friends, but he hadn't called me once since that night at the movie. How fickle boys could be!

Dad was in a quiet mood, and Max and I both noticed it after five minutes.

"What's up for tonight, Dad?" I asked, trying to snap him out of his mood. "Are we going to eat with Julie?"

"No." Dad was still quiet, but at least he was willing to tell us why. He smiled, but his eyes were sad. "Julie and I aren't seeing each other any more."

"Oh." I didn't know what else to say. "Is that good or bad?"

"Oh, I'm sure it's for the best," Dad answered, pulling into the parking lot at his condo on the beach. "And we'll have a great weekend with just the three of us."

While Max and I moved our stuff in, Dad took off for a walk down the beach. "He's really in a mood," I told Max.

"Melancholy," Max answered. "A totally useless waste of energy. I'm surprised he's letting it get a hold of him."

"Max, everybody feels depressed sometimes," I explained. "Not everyone is as without emotion as you pretend to be."

Max actually looked hurt, and I ran my fingers through his curly hair. "Sorry, kiddo. We'll just do our best to cheer him up, OK?"

For Operation Cheer Up, we asked Dad to take us to eat at the Fluorescent Coffee House, a sixties restaurant. We were munching away on burgers and fries and listening to the Supremes, when somebody pushed the button for "Up-Up and Away" on the jukebox.

I thought the song would be romantic and pretty, like Mom had sung it, but I was surprised at how lively it was. It perked Dad up right away, too. Soon he was singing into the salt shaker and kicking his legs under the table in one of his weird little dances. Max and I just looked at each other and snickered. Dad could really be crazy when he wanted to be.

"Up-Up and Away" was replaced by something slower and softer, and Dad's mood changed just about as quickly. "Those were the days," he said, more to himself than to us. "We thought we could fly through anything."

I didn't want him to sink into melancholy again. "Hey Dad, Mom says you used to sing to her all the time. Why didn't you ever sing in public? You've got a good voice."

Dad had been staring out across the room, but he looked at me and laughed. "Thanks, gypsy girl. But I did sing in public once, and that was enough for me."

"Why only once? Did you get stage fright or something?" Max wanted to know.

"No, I did well, or so they tell me," Dad answered, viciously stabbing a French fry with his fork. "I had been chosen out of my entire high school to sing our school song for the governor at our county fair. I was only fourteen. It was a big honor, and I worked my tail off to get ready for it."

He took another bite, and I was afraid he wouldn't finish the story. "What happened?"

Dad swallowed, then took a sip of his drink. "I sang—in front of the governor and about ten thousand people. I did the best I could, poured my heart into it."

He took another bite, and this time Max prompted him.

"So what happened? Didn't the governor like you?"

Dad swallowed, then took his napkin and neatly wiped his mouth. He leaned back, crossed his arms, and looked at us. Finally he said, "They laughed."

"They . . . laughed?"

"Yes. I didn't know it at the time, but behind and above my stage, a group of performing monkeys was doing a show for another crowd. The people in my audience were so busy watching and laughing at the monkeys, they ignored me. Even the governor was bent over double, laughing at the monkeys."

He looked down at the floor and shadows covered his face. "I wish they had thrown tomatoes instead. To do a bad job and get booed—that's one thing. To do your best and be ignored—that's worse. I came off that stage and swore I'd never sing in public again."

So that was it. My father had his heart broken by people who didn't care or see what he had invested in his music. From that day on, he had never sung except to people who cared about him. Who wouldn't ignore him.

Finally I understood why he didn't want me to risk my heart in the audition.

Dad gave me a lot to think about, and that night when I went to my room, I pulled my private notebook out of my suitcase. I wanted to write a poem for Dad, and maybe someday I'd even show it to him.

Little boy at the fair,
Have you stopped to look where
Your dreams have taken you now?
You've worked very long
On your beautiful song,
And you're ready to take your bow.

Young man at the fair,
Don't stop to look there,
Keep your eyes on the future so bright.
If you get burdened down
And feel like a clown,
You'll go away sad in the night.

Old man at the fair,
Have you thought about where
You left your dreams on the way?
Look around at your side,
Your talents may hide
In your children—let them have their day.

When I was finished, I knew I'd never show the poem to Dad. Who was I to lecture him? He'd only say I was trying to make him feel bad about not paying my tuition for the Spa, and I honestly wasn't trying to put him on a guilt trip. I closed my notebook and slipped it under my pillow.

I was almost asleep when I heard Max whisper, "Hey, Cass, are you awake?"

"Yeah, come in," I answered. Max came in, dressed in Dad's too-big pajamas. He looked like the little boy in my poem, or at least how I thought the little boy would look. I thought for a minute about showing the poem to Max, but decided he wouldn't understand.

I put my head back down on my pillow and yawned. "What's up?"

"Do you want to hear about my experiment?" Max was bursting with excitement. "I'm really close. I think I've finally licked the problem of taste. Suki's been helping me."

I raised my head and glared at him. "Suki? What have you been doing to my dog?"

"Nothing." Max looked offended. "But I've developed a dog-food formula with algae ingredients, and the food is chemically more nutritious and more economical to produce than the dog foods with animal by-products. This could be revolutionary for dog-food manufacturers! Think of it! Algae treats, algae chews! All I do is grow the algae, spin it in a centrifuge, grind it with a mortar and pestle, and bake. Chorella seems to be the best species, so far, at least, but I'm also going to try other varieties. . . ."

I didn't hear any more. I fell asleep on poor Max.

13

The next morning Dad seemed to be in a better mood. "What a nice day," he said after opening the blinds that covered his balcony and beach view. "Great day for a picnic."

"Sure is," I agreed, pouring myself a bowl of cereal. "What did you have in mind?"

Dad had never been very subtle with his hints. "What's your mother doing today?"

I went to the refrigerator. Did Dad know about Mom dating Tom Harris? Had Max mentioned that she was having Tom over for dinner tonight?

"I don't know what she's doing today," I answered truthfully, pulling out a pitcher of orange juice. "Probably the same old stuff. She's taking aerobics and tennis lessons again. She has some new clients, too, so she's pretty busy."

"Oh," he said, nodding. "Do you think she's busy tonight?"

What was he doing? A couple of months ago I'd have been overjoyed if Dad had wanted to see Mom for any reason at all, but his timing was lousy. Had hearing "Up-Up and Away" made him think about old times?

For a minute I thought that I could really get Mom in hot water if I sent Dad over there tonight while Tom Harris was at our house. That'd serve her right somehow. But Mom would kill me, Dad would either get mad or be even more hurt, and Tom Harris would probably just sit there being charming. I decided it wasn't worth it.

"She's busy tonight, Dad," I said, as gently as I could. I might as well tell him everything. "She has a date."

He looked out the window again, then made a weak excuse. "Well, I guess I can't drop off that support check tonight, can I?"

"You can give it to me," I reminded him. "And Max has some mail for you, too." I looked out into the living room. "Where is the whiz kid?"

"He was up late working on his project," Dad answered, coming into the kitchen to get his coffee. "He says he's near a breakthrough."

"That's right. I remember." I took my cereal and sat down at the table across from Dad. "Speaking of breakthroughs, Dad, my audition for the performance arts school is in two weeks."

He frowned. "Don't tell me you're going through with it."

I nodded. "I'm going for the scholarship that's available. I'm not like Max, Dad. I didn't get your brain. I got your music, and I want to use it."

He sipped his coffee, still frowning. "I don't agree with what you're doing," he said, blowing across his hot coffee, "but I guess that's your mother's decision."

I stirred my cereal. "The audition is open to the public, on July 7, a Saturday. Can you come?"

It was just a hopeful question because I already knew the answer. He and Max would be on their summer trip on the seventh, but I hoped he'd say he was sorry he'd miss it, or he would have liked to come, or that he'd be thinking of me. Instead he pushed back his chair, stood up, and said, "Can't." He put his coffee mug in the sink and left the room.

I had lost my appetite. The young man at the fair had turned into a bitter old man who gave me his voice and didn't want me to use it.

That afternoon Max took a break from his experiment to challenge Dad to a computer game, and I went to the small guest room where I slept on a rollaway bed when I visited Dad. I figured I might as well practice, since there were only thirteen days until the audition. I pulled out my copy of "Villanelle" and tossed it aside. I didn't have a piano here, and I didn't think Dad would appreciate me screeching the high notes while he and Max were concentrating on that dumb computer game.

But I spread the music to "I Enjoy Being a Girl" out on the bed and stood next to it. I had the song memorized and could sing it quietly under my breath while I worked on some sort of actions to put with the song. Coming up with choreography was harder than I thought it would be. I made all sorts of cute gestures in the air and checked myself in the mirror, but after two verses the gestures felt unnatural and I felt stupid. After twenty minutes of making the same dumb gestures over and over again, I plopped down on the bed in discouragement. I wished I had gone to Andrea for her help. She would have had good ideas, but I would have had to listen to her talk about Chip.

I wanted to talk to somebody. I could have called Andrea and made everything all right again, but she'd be sure to mention that she and Chip were going somewhere or doing something, and I wasn't in the mood to hear that everyone was having good times but me. I would have called Chip, but now that he and Andrea were going together, she'd have a jealous fit if I called him. I could have called Nick, but I really didn't feel comfortable calling him. What if I interrupted him from doing something important? Worse yet, what if he wasn't home and I had to talk to his dad or to his Uncle Jacob? How embarrassing! Or what if he was home but he didn't want to talk to me?

"Don't set yourself up for rejection," I told my reflection in the mirror. So I went out into the kitchen and called Mr. Williams.

There was a smile in his voice this time. "I'm glad to hear the songs are going well," he said. "Are you comfortable with them?"

"The first song is no problem," I told him, "but 'Villanelle' is something else. It's been a real challenge."

"Well, keep working on it," Mr. Williams said. "You should never go to an audition with only one song prepared. You never know when they'll need to hear more."

"That's just it," I answered. "I was wondering if we could get together again so you could give me some pointers. I'm not doing anything next week."

"Ah, Cassie, I'm sorry," he said, but he didn't sound very sorry. "I don't have a spare minute this week because I'm getting married a week from today. And then I'm off on my honeymoon for a month. But don't you worry—just do your best and you'll do fine."

"OK." My last hope went down the drain. "Uh, congratulations on your wedding, and have a nice honeymoon."

"Thanks," Mr. Williams said. "Good luck."

"I'll need it." I hung up and sat looking at the phone. I had set myself up for rejection anyway. Mr. Williams had really let me down.

Max would say it was stupid of me to feel that way. After all, who was Mr. Williams? Just a teacher who had helped me out, given me confidence, and sent me on my way. I was grateful to him for all that. But he was also a man with his own private life. He wasn't my father or my personal coach. He cared about me no more and no less than he cared about all his students.

I went back to the guest room and hoped the hours would pass quickly so I could go home again. Suki, at least, was home. There was no one else to turn to when I really needed help.

14

Back home on Monday morning, I decided the only person I could rely on was myself. Mr. Williams had said to do my best, and that's what I was going to do. I was going to learn those songs the best I could, even that dumb "Villa-nelle," and I was going to get into the Central Florida School for Performing Arts. Getting in would be no problem, I could certainly win at least a slot. But how could I come up with ten thousand dollars for the tuition if I didn't win the scholarship?

In my private notebook I made a list of every-one I knew who either loved me or had money. Mom was at the top—she loved me, and she wanted me to go to the school, but she simply couldn't afford it. I wrote *no* by her name.

Dad—well, he loved me, but he didn't want me to go to the school, and maybe he couldn't even afford it. I had always thought of my dad as well-off, but last night before he brought us home he'd mentioned something about the high cost of living and how hard it was to make payments on his condo plus help Mom with the payments on our house. Ten thousand dollars was a lot of money. Maybe Dad didn't even have that kind of cash to spare. *No* I wrote reluctantly by his name.

Mr. Harris—well, he didn't love me, but he probably would like me to go to the Spa because it would please Mom, and he was rich. But I didn't like him, and I'd rather go to Astronaut High than be indebted to him. That wouldn't be fair to Mom, either. If somehow he gave me the money, it'd be hard for her to dump him when the time came. *No way* I wrote by his name.

My grandparents were living on a fixed income. They couldn't help me out. I scratched their names off. The only other names on the list were Chip and Andrea, who loved each other, Max, and Suki. Three kids and a dog with probably not twenty dollars between them.

You see there, I told myself, *if you need the money, you're going to have to get it yourself.* Would a bank give an almost-fourteen-year-old girl a loan for ten thousand dollars? No. Could I earn that much from baby-sitting or delivering papers or selling myself as a housemaid after school? No. Did I know any rich old people who might mention me in their will? No. Did I have anything to sell? Any savings bonds hidden away? Any stocks in my name? No, no, and no.

I pictured myself passing the audition and then throwing myself at the feet of the elegant Mrs. Allan. "Please, I'll scrub floors, clean windows, and serve lunch every day if you'll just let me come to school here!" She'd pull back from such an emotional display, of course, and laugh her tinkling laugh. "Only those who are very well-connected or very deserving win scholarships," she'd say. "You have just an ordinary talent, just singing. You probably can't even scrub floors well."

I tore my list pages out of my private notebook, wadded them up, and threw them across the room. It was hopeless. I went to the kitchen and hoped that Max wouldn't be too busy to talk to me.

The kitchen looked like a kitchen again; all the laboratory stuff was gone. Max was sitting at the kitchen bar with an untouched plate of Twinkies in front of him. He was writing on a notecard, his forehead wrinkled in concentration. I peeked over the counter and was surprised to see that he was wearing his best navy blue dress pants, a white shirt, and a red tie.

"Aren't you going to eat your Twinkies?" I asked. "And what outfit is that? An early Fourth of July special?"

Max didn't even look up. "It's not an outfit at all," he explained, still writing. "It's real clothes. I have an appointment."

"An appointment? Where, at the mayor's office? Why are you dressed like the flag?"

Mom came into the kitchen wearing her business suit. "We're going to the American Healthwise Food Company," she explained, clipping on her best earrings. "I can't believe Max didn't tell you about this."

"I tried to tell her a couple of times," Max said, still writing on his notecard. "But she fell asleep on me once, and she's been too busy to listen."

I felt guilty. "I'm sorry, OK? But what's this all about? Tell me now."

"Max has invented a new recipe for dog food," Mom explained, looking for her purse. "A couple of weeks ago he wrote the president of the Healthwise Food Company, and they want to meet with him today. They may be interested in buying Max's formula!"

Max looked up. "Green Grub," he said, "or Fido's Fricassee. But you're not interested."

"I am," I assured him. "But I'm not much into algae."

Max pointed to his notes. "Most high-protein dog foods contain not less than 27 percent protein and not more than 12 percent moisture, OK?" I nodded. "Well, Green Grub has taken out the moisture, or most of it, by a process of spinning the algae and dehydrating the dog mix. By this method I can increase the protein dramatically, add additional nutrients, eliminate the

116

need for expensive animal by-products, and decrease the moisture. Follow me?"

I nodded again, but I was beginning to feel lost.

"The rest of the formula is the usual mixture of fat, fiber, calcium, and phosphorous," he said, "but the important difference is the algae. It's cheap, easy to grow, and vitamin-rich. When the customer adds a little water, the mix plumps out, and the dog has a delicious dinner."

"Ugh," I said, shaking my head. "But congratulations. I hope the company buys it." I pointed at his notecards. "Is that the recipe?"

"Yep," Max finished and put the notecards in his pocket. "And here are the samples." He reached for one of Mom's plastic storage containers, and in it I could see several pebbly pieces of dog food, all faintly green.

"It looks great," I said weakly.

"It will be great," Max said. "And if the idea takes off, they can make dog bones, snacks, and an entire line of cat food, too. I'll call that one Feline Feast."

"We'd better go, Max," Mom said, digging for her car keys. "Cassie, we'll be back in an hour or two. Let me know if anyone calls, OK?" There was more than a glow of hope in her eyes. "Like Mr. Harris."

I nodded, and Max made a grab for the Twinkies. "For the road," he said, and I threw a napkin in his direction as he walked out the door.

"For the mess," I added. "Come back rich, OK?"

While they were gone, I swallowed my pride and called Andrea. "Want to come over today?"

"Oh, I don't know," she said breezily. "There's a lot to do around here today. I'm supposed to go swimming this afternoon, and Chip may call."

"Well, OK." I could tell she was still mad. "Listen, I wanted to say I'm sorry for giving you the brush-off the other day. I've just had a lot on my mind with this audition and all."

"No problem. But Cassie, I've got to go, OK?"

"OK."

She hung up.

I was in front of the mirror in my room, trying once again to come up with some decent moves for "I Enjoy Being a Girl" when the doorbell rang.

Andrea stood there. "So how does it feel to get the brush-off?" she asked.

"Not good," I admitted. "I'm sorry, OK? I shouldn't have treated you that way."

"You're forgiven." She smiled. "So can I come in, or what?"

"Sure." I opened the door wider. "But what if you miss Chip's call? And weren't you supposed to go swimming?"

She winked and smiled. "Chip can always call back, and I can always swim. But it's been days since I talked to my best friend."

I made a mental note not to mention Chip

for the rest of the day. If I was still Andrea's best friend, then I hadn't lost everything. Chip would probably never confide in me again, but at least I could talk to Andrea.

"As a matter of fact," I said as I pulled her through the hall, "I really need you. If you're not too mad at me, could you help me learn some steps or something for this song? I feel like an albatross."

We worked in front of the mirror for an hour. Andrea has a natural flair for movement, and she walked through the song and added movements as naturally as breathing. By lunchtime, I had hope again.

"Whatever you do, act like you really mean to do it," Andrea reminded me. "If you look confident, you'll *be* confident."

"No, I won't. I'll be terrified!" We laughed, and I led the way to the kitchen. "Want a drink? I'm thirsty."

"Sure." Andrea noticed Max's pile of scribbled notes on the counter. "Max must be home," she said. "What's this? The formula for an atomic bomb?"

"You won't believe it. He's home all week because he and Dad leave Friday for their trip. But now he and Mom are down at the American Healthwise Food Company trying to sell one of his experiments. Get this—he calls it Green Grub, dog food made from algae."

"You're kidding." Andrea's blue eyes were open wide. She shook her head. "You're so lucky to have a little brother who's useful. My brother is nothing but a pest."

"Max is all right," I admitted, pouring two glasses of lemonade. "I'll miss him when he and Dad leave."

Andrea took her glass from me and took a sip. "How much would they pay for his experiment, anyway?"

"I don't know." I frowned. "A few hundred dollars, maybe? Max would love that. He could buy that chemistry set he's always asking for."

"A few hundred?" Andrea laughed. "Cassie, you're ignorant. Big companies like Healthwise pay thousands for things like that. Maybe even millions."

I stared at Max's messy pile of notes. This morning I had been beating my brain to think of someone who could provide me with ten thousand dollars for tuition, and all along my little brother had been sitting on a million-dollar recipe for Green Grub.

15

When I heard the key turn in the lock, I flew to the kitchen door. Mom and Max came in, all smiles. "What took so long?" I asked, breathless. "You've been gone three hours!"

Max grinned. "Mr. McCabe, the president, took us to lunch," he said. "And then we had to sign papers, and I toured their lab and production facility."

Mom sank onto a kitchen stool. "It was exciting," she said, bobbing her head so enthusiastically that her short hair bounced. "Really incredible."

"So?" I asked, pulling up a stool. "So you sold it, right? For how much?"

"Really, Cassie." Mom frowned, but her eyes were still dancing. "Is money all you think about?"

"Yes," I answered. "Max, what's the deal?"

Max hopped up onto a stool at the kitchen bar. "Upon my graduation from college, I get an immediate position as a vice president if I want it," he announced solemnly. "And they'll pay my way to college if I promise to work for them after graduation."

I sniffed. "That's nothing. You don't want to make dog food all your life, do you? What did they give you *now?*"

Mom laughed. "That's not nothing, Cassie. That's really quite a lot."

Max went on, counting on his fingers. "Well, that was two things. Another thing is I can work in their lab any time I want, as long as I don't blow anything up." He looked up and smiled. "I like that part best, actually."

I groaned. "Go on, keep counting."

He pointed to his fourth finger. "I can buy American Healthwise products wholesale. You should like that, Cassie. Suki will be eating *good.*"

"Enough, already. What else?"

Max shrugged and touched his pinky. "That's about it. Except for a twenty-thousand-dollar check."

Mom tilted her head back and cackled with delight while Max beamed at me. But I was disappointed. Only twenty thousand dollars? I was expecting at least half a million. "That's all?"

"What do you mean?" Mom stopped laughing and glared at me. "That's amazing. How many nine year olds do you know who earn twenty thousand dollars in the first month of summer?" She walked over to Max, grabbed his head with her hands, and kissed his brown hair. "Max Brian Perkins, I'm proud of you," she said. She walked away then, humming happily, but she popped her head back into the kitchen to ask, "Cass? Any calls for me?"

"No, Mom," I sighed. "Mr. Harris didn't call."

She laughed. "Then I'll have to call him," she said. "News like this can't wait. Besides, he'll know how to put Max's money in a trust fund."

When she had gone, I looked at Max. "A trust fund?" I asked, looking doubtful. "Are you sure you want to put your money in a trust fund? Don't you want to *use* any of it?"

Max shrugged. "What would I spend it on? Permission to use the lab at the company is all I really wanted."

"Just think, Max," I said, leaning toward him. "Isn't there a new computer you'd like to try? Or a trip you want to take? You and Dad could fly to all those places you want to visit this summer instead of riding in a hot car."

"I want to ride with Dad," Max insisted. "If we flew everywhere, our trip would be over in a week."

I felt a little guilty about badgering him, but honestly, Max was being perfectly dense! "Don't you want to keep some money out? You never know when something might come up."

"Like what?" Max's eyes narrowed suspiciously.

"Like, maybe your sister won't win the scholarship she needs," I blurted out. "And you could keep out some money to loan her if she needs it."

Max looked at me in surprise. "You want my money?"

"I *need* your money, Max," I explained, "or at least I might. But I'll pay you back one day when I'm successful, I promise."

"I don't know, Cassie," Max said with a shake of his head. "Mom may not let me loan it to you. She wants me to invest it for the future. That seems to be the most logical thing to do."

"Max Brian Perkins!" I crossed my arms in disapproval. "After all I've done for you!"

"What?" For the first time in my life, I saw distrust in Max's brown eyes. "I wanted you to help me with my experiment, and you wouldn't. I had planned for you and me to go together to Healthwise and to use Suki as proof that dogs like Green Grub. But you wouldn't. You wouldn't even talk to me because you were too worried about your boyfriends and your stupid singing."

Max had never spoken to me like this.

"You've got some nerve, Cassie, to ask for my money now. You're just using me the same way you've been using everyone else. You can't ignore people until you need something and then expect them to jump when you ask them to."

I couldn't have been more surprised if Suki had suddenly started to lecture me. I slipped off my stool and went into the garage, leaving Max in the kitchen. He could have his moment of glory. He deserved it. But he could have it alone.

I grabbed my bike and coasted down the driveway. I couldn't forget the horrible things Max had said, and worst of all, I was beginning to realize they were true. What had I done for anyone this summer besides myself? Not one thing.

I pedaled furiously, not knowing where to go. But I didn't care.

At first I simply pedaled out of my subdivision and headed down Canova Cove's main road, thinking as I pedaled. Max was right, I had tried to use him just as I had used Andrea. A sneaking suspicion nagged at me—had I even tried to use Chip that night at the movie to make Nick jealous? I could have easily suggested that Nick sit by Andrea, but I had wanted to keep that option open myself. It had been a selfish thing to do.

The only person I hadn't hurt lately was Nick. Even though his neighborhood was five or six miles away, I headed in that direction. I knew that as long as Mr. Harris was dating my mother, he wouldn't object to my coming over to visit. He might even be flattered and think I was coming to visit him.

I stopped at a 7-Eleven to call and tell Mom I was out riding my bike and I'd be home by dinnertime. No sense in having her worry. After

I hung up I looked through the phone book to find Nick's address: 101 Falcon Circle.

Falcon Circle was a circular road near the river, and the cool breeze off the water felt good as I pedaled along under the hot sun. I would be sweaty when I got there, but at least the white cotton shorts and pink shirt I was wearing looked nice. Nick would either be happy, embarrassed, or aggravated about my showing up. I'd take a chance and just hope he'd be glad.

The house at 101 Falcon Circle was a two-story Swiss-chalet type, unusual for Florida. The thick green lawn was wide, and a circular driveway led to a three-car garage with two cars parked inside. I recognized Mr. Harris's black Mercedes, and a blue convertible sports car was parked inside, too. "That's probably for the day Nick turns sixteen," I mumbled to myself. "It must be nice to get everything you want."

I parked my bike, smoothed my shorts, gathered my courage, and rang the doorbell. I waited about ten seconds, decided the whole thing was a bad idea, and was just about to leave when the door opened. "Yes?" barked a dark-haired man in reading glasses. "Didn't we pay you for the paper already?"

"I'm not the paper carrier," I stammered. "I came to see if Nick was home. I'm Cassie Perkins."

"Perkins." The man considered my name, and then the corners of his eyes smiled, even though his mouth didn't. His lips and teeth were too busy clenching an unlit cigar.

"So you're *her* daughter," he said, opening the door wider. "Well, you may as well come in. I'll get Nick for you."

He left me in a cool bricked foyer while he walked to the bottom of the staircase. I expected him to walk up the stairs like some sort of butler and bring Nick down, but he just opened his lips and, through clenched teeth, bellowed, "Nick! Company for you!"

I looked down at the floor, embarrassed, but after a few minutes I heard rumblings from upstairs and saw Nick's head over the banister.

"Who is it?" he called. But then he saw me.

"Hi," I said.

"Well, hi, Cassie," he answered, galloping on down the stairs.

"Button your shirt and comb your hair," the dark-haired man commanded as Nick passed him. "You've got company, for heaven's sake."

Nick smiled and buttoned the brightly flowered shirt he was wearing over his shorts. "I see you've met Uncle Jacob."

I nodded. "Sort of."

"What a surprise." Nick looked me over. "Did you walk?"

"No, I sort of surprised myself. I won't stay. I was just riding my bike and thought I'd drop in to say hi."

"It's OK. Uncle Jacob, is there anything to drink?" Nick turned to his uncle, who was still standing at the foot of the stairs like a wooden Indian, staring at us.

"There're cold drinks in the little fridge by the pool and fruit in the fridge," Uncle Jacob said. "But don't go fillin' up on junk! And don't make a mess."

Nick took my arm and led me into the kitchen. "Don't mind Uncle Jacob," he whispered. "His bark's worse than his bite." I glanced over my shoulder and saw Uncle Jacob retreat into a little room with bookshelves, a table, a typewriter, and about a hundred wads of crumpled paper on the floor.

Nick took a bowl of fruit out of the refrigerator. "Grab a couple of glasses out of that cupboard by the sink, will you?" he called. "The drinks are out by the pool." Like a little helper, I followed him, glad for once that somebody was telling me what to do and not making me stop to figure it out for myself.

We relaxed on lounge chairs by the pool, and after about five minutes I found my tongue and began to tell Nick everything—how much I wanted to go to the Spa, how hard the songs had been, how frustrated I was with my father, how my mother was driving me crazy with her happy humming, and how Max made me feel terrible for wanting a loan.

But Nick just looked at me. "Do you want to swim?" he asked when I had finished. "I could ask Uncle Jacob to go to your house and pick up your bathing suit."

Hadn't he heard a word I'd said? I was pouring my heart out to him, and all he could think about was having Uncle Jacob run to my house for my suit! "No, I don't want to swim," I said quietly, "and I wouldn't ask your uncle to run all the way to my house. I'm sure he has better things to do."

"He wouldn't mind," Nick shrugged. "He's not doing anything important."

"He's working," I said. "I saw him going to his typewriter. From the looks of the mess, he's not doing very well, either."

"Then he needs a break," Nick said, standing up and stretching. "I want to swim, and I want you to come, too." He put his hand out to help me up from the chaise lounge. "Come on, let's go ask him."

"No, thank you." I put my hands down on the lounge and pushed myself up, ignoring his outstretched hand. "I can't just order people around—that's what's been getting me into trouble all along."

Nick looked confused.

"I've got to go, anyway," I said, smoothing my wrinkled shorts again. "Thanks for the drink. I'll see you later."

I turned to leave. Nick didn't say anything, but there was a loud splash from the pool.

16

Dinner was on the table when I got home. I was almost too tired and hot to eat, but Mom had actually gone to the trouble of making pancakes, so I thought I'd try to eat just one.

She was in an incredibly good mood. "I have good news for both of you," she said after Max and I sat down. "I talked to Tom, and he's arranged everything. Max, he's going to put your money into a trust fund, and you will have access to the interest earnings every year, or even every month if you need some money. That way you'll have money when you need it, but the principal amount will be held for you until you're ready to be on your own."

She turned to me next. "Cassie, I know how much you want to go to the performance arts school. Tom said he can arrange with Mrs. Allan to give you a scholarship. Your worries are over."

I choked on the pancake. "That's not right," I said, not believing it could be so easy. "You're supposed to win a scholarship because you deserve it, not because somebody paid for it!"

Mom rolled her eyes. "You don't understand," she said. "It wouldn't be the Constance Hamilton Scholarship you've been hoping for. Tom will simply donate your tuition money to the school. It's a business deal."

"I don't understand."

Mom shrugged. "Instead of paying me for redecorating his law offices, Tom is paying your tuition money for the school. It's really simple. He says that way he can keep me around to update the decor throughout the year." She laughed. "Isn't that sweet?"

"Mom, you can't do that. You need that money for us to live on."

"I thought I would, too, but I'm getting so many referrals from my work in the law office that my business will still do quite nicely next year. Don't worry, Cassie. We'll all do fine."

Mom was actually smiling as if this news was supposed to make me happy. I couldn't believe it. It felt like cheating to me. I'd never be able to tell anyone I'd won a scholarship knowing the whole thing was set up by my mother's boyfriend. I wouldn't feel proud about going to the Spa. Plus, I didn't want to owe anything to Tom Harris. He was just like his son, someone who thought he could get anything by paying for it.

I shook my head in disgust. "Mother, how can you go out with *him?* He's a snob."

Mom's face turned violently red, and she slowly raised her arm and pointed toward the hallway. "You may go to your room," she said, her arm shaking with her anger. "And I'll thank you to keep your opinions to yourself."

"Well, I won't take his money," I yelled as I rushed past her. "I'd rather go to school in Tasmania than have him buy my scholarship."

Later, in the exile of my room, the phone rang, and I lifted my extension. It was Dad. "Hi, gypsy girl," he said. "How's everything?"

"It's either great or terrible, depending on who you ask," I answered. "Max sold his experiment, so he's great. Mom's dating a snob that I hate, and that's terrible. But I'm not allowed to say anything bad about him."

"Oh." Dad was quiet, and I was afraid I had put him in one of his melancholy moods. "Well," he spoke slowly, "I just called to tell Max that I'd pick him up at eight o'clock on Friday morning for our trip. That'll be OK, won't it?"

"Yeah. He's looking forward to it."

We stayed on the line for about two minutes without saying anything.

"Are you OK?" I asked finally.

"Yeah," Dad answered. "Are you?"

"I'll survive." I wanted to tell him everything, but he certainly was in no mood to give me advice.

"Well, see you later," he said.

"OK, Dad. I love you."

133

17

Thursday night I dreamed that I was at the
audition, trying to sing on a tightrope while
holding a cigar in my mouth while Max and
a legion of green dogs stood off to the side
watching silently. It was a genuine nightmare.
Every time I'd open my mouth to sing, I'd
remember that I had to hold on to the cigar
and keep my balance, and whenever I looked
around for help, the only person nearby was
Max. But I couldn't get to him because he was
guarded by big, green dogs.

"So long, Cassie," he said when I started to
fall, and then I opened my eyes and wasn't
dreaming anymore. It was Friday morning, and
Dad was at the house to pick Max up for their
trip. I sat up and saw Max, already dressed,
standing in the doorway. "Dad's here, and we're
ready to go," he said.

"Wait a minute, let me get awake," I muttered, shaking the sleepiness out of my head. Next to his big suitcase, Max looked a little small and even a little afraid. "I hope you have a good trip."

"Me, too." Max turned to leave, so I jumped out of bed and grabbed his arm. "Wait a minute. I wanted to tell you I'm sorry. I was wrong to ask for your money. It's your money, you worked hard to earn it, and I had no business asking for it."

Max looked down at his tennis shoes, but then he looked up and smiled at me. "You can do it, Cass," he said. "You don't need my money or anyone else's. You can win that scholarship all by yourself."

I leaned against the door frame. "I don't know, kiddo, but I'll try, OK? Give me a call next weekend, and I'll tell you how it went."

"OK." Dad hollered from the living room that it was time to go. "I gotta go," Max said, looking up and not moving.

"OK." I reached out and gave him an awkward hug. "Say a prayer for me on Saturday, will ya?"

Max nodded, picked up his suitcase, and went down the hall to meet Dad. I padded down the hall after him and peeked into the living room. Dad stood there, his hands on Max's shoulders, while Mom fussed that Dad should make sure Max ate three meals a day and to call her if he got sick.

Dad held up his hand, "Yeah, yeah," he said.

"Don't worry." As they walked out the door, Dad glanced toward the hall and saw me. He waved. "So long, Cassie. See you in five or six weeks." That was all.

I went back to bed. I was getting used to my father and brother walking in and out of my life. The phone rang, but I didn't answer it, and in a little while I went to sleep again, but this time I didn't dream.

Mom woke me up a little later. She sat on my bed and literally bounced up and down until I opened one eye and looked to see if we were having an earthquake.

"Get up," she trilled. "Pack your overnight bag. We're going away for the weekend."

"What?" I mumbled, sitting up. "I don't want to go away. I want to go back to sleep."

"Nonsense," Mom said, hopping up and opening my closet. "Ugh, this is a disaster area. Cass, honey, you've simply got to take better care of your things." She shuffled through the hangers. "Where's that darling red and white sundress we got you last summer?"

"I outgrew it last fall," I answered, pulling my hair out of my eyes. "I bloomed, remember?"

"Oh yes." She chuckled. "Well, we don't have time to go shopping, so I guess we'll have to make do with what you've got in here. Pack three shorts outfits, a couple of sundresses, and of course, your bathing suit." She crinkled her forehead. "Do you have two?"

"You said we couldn't afford two."

"I remember." She ran her hand through her hair. "Well, maybe we can pick something up for you at the beach."

"Wait a minute." I swung my legs out from under the covers and put them on the floor. "Where are we going, why are we going, and who are we going with?"

"With whom are we going," Mom corrected me. "Don't end your sentences with a preposition. Don't they teach you anything in school these days?"

"OK, with whom are we going? And where are you getting the money to pay for all this?"

She sat down next to me. "We're going to a beach house for the weekend as guests of Tom and Nick. You can even bring the dog. It'll be fun."

Ugh. I turned my head so she wouldn't see how repelled I was by the whole idea, but she was back at the closet trying to coordinate at least three decent outfits for me.

"Mom, we can't do that."

"Why not?"

"We can't go away with a strange man. This isn't a family vacation! Sleeping in the same house? That's gross!" I shuddered. Could I walk around in my nightshirt in front of Tom Harris? Use the same bathroom? Park my toothbrush next to his? Never!

I tried a new tactic: "Anyway, what would people think?"

"People won't think anything because it's

perfectly innocent." Mom smoothed out my bedspread so she could lay out my clothes. "Everyone will know it's innocent because we're bringing you and Nick along. Uncle Jacob is coming, too, so I won't have to cook."

"Uncle Jacob?" I could just imagine him walking down the beach in dark socks, sandals, plaid shorts, a white shirt, and his unlit cigar.

"Yes. Tom's getting a lovely three-bedroom place. And he's picking us up right after lunch, so you need to get up and get busy." She paused a minute and checked her fingernails. "If you hurry, we can get to Burdines and get each of us a new bathing suit before lunch. Doesn't that sound good?"

Mom would have a fit if she knew I was wasting time on the phone, so I talked quietly. "Andrea?"

"Cassie?" she giggled. "Why are you whispering?"

"Because I'm supposed to be packing. What would you say if someone told you they were going away for the weekend with their boyfriend?"

She shrieked. "You're running away with Nick?"

"No, dummy. My mother's going away with Tom Harris."

"Oh." She was quiet. "You're kidding, right? Your mother's not the type for a romantic rendezvous."

"It's not going to be romantic. Nick and I and Uncle Jacob are going, too."

Andrea sighed. "Cassie, you really had me going. I thought it was going to be something really racy, but since everybody's going, it's more like a family vacation, isn't it?"

"We're *not* a family."

"Don't get bent out of shape." Andrea snorted. "You beat everything, Cassie Perkins. If you like Nick so much, you should be on cloud nine."

"Well, I'm not, OK?" I snapped.

"Hey, don't take my head off."

I groaned. It wasn't Andrea's fault. "I'm sorry. I guess I should be excited, but Max and Dad left this morning, I'm worried about my audition next weekend, and I'm just confused."

"Don't worry about it," Andrea said. "Everything will be fine, and you'll have fun. Just call me when you get back in. I can't wait to hear about this!"

The beach house made Dad's condo look like a slum. It was more like an estate on stilts than a weekly rental, and inside it was so plush and closed in I wondered why they bothered to build it on the beach. Thick, heavy drapes hid the ocean view, and a gurgling fountain in the indoor patio drowned out the soothing sound of the ocean waves. There was even a Jacuzzi in the main bathroom, so you could soak indoors instead of out in the sun.

"Why didn't they put a pool in the living

room?" I asked Mom as we looked around. "Then you wouldn't have to even *swim* in the Atlantic."

She glared at me. "Hush."

I shrugged and took my music folder into the bedroom Mom and I would share. Nick and Mr. Harris would have a room down the hall, and Uncle Jacob's room was right across from us. I wouldn't have to worry about Tom Harris's toothbrush. His room had a private bath.

Uncle Jacob was checking out the groceries he'd had delivered earlier that morning. "Hey, Cassie, do ya like lobster tails?" he growled as I went by.

"Hey, Uncle Jacob," I growled back. "I likes 'em a lot."

To my surprise, he smiled and nearly dropped his cigar.

I perched on one of the stools at the bar. "Why do you carry that thing around, anyway?"

He pursed his lips around the cigar. "Stopped smokin' years ago. But couldn't get out of the habit of having something in my mouth. I figured it was either this or a lollipop." He leaned over the counter toward me. "Now which do you figure is bettah?"

I winked at him. "You could get a pacifier."

"Ha!"

Jacob trumpeted so loudly that Mom stuck her head into the kitchen. "Everything OK in here?" she asked, a flicker of doubt on her face. "Cassie, you're not in Uncle Jacob's way are you?"

"No, Mom, I'm not," I answered.

"She's a pain in the behind," Jacob snarled, and when Mom looked startled, he added, "but she can hang around my kitchen anytime."

Mom backed out cautiously, probably afraid Jacob would start yelling at her. But I was beginning to feel as though I'd found a friend.

"Nick tells me you're a writer," I ventured, not looking at him.

"Oh yeah?" He muttered, searching through the cabinets. "I don't know whatever gave him that idea."

"He says you write columns. I figured you must be pretty good."

"Where's the confounded broiler?" He didn't answer me, but I knew he wouldn't.

"I write, too."

He stopped slamming doors and looked at me. "And I suppose you want me to read your stuff?"

"No." I pretended to study my fingernails. "I don't let anybody read my stuff. It's private."

He bit down so hard on his cigar that the end of it swung up and nearly hit him in the nose. "How d'ya expect to be a writer without readers?" he snapped. "D'ya think it's a one-way street?"

He had a frying pan in his hand, and he held it above his head. I had to steel myself not to duck.

"Writin' without readers isn't writin', but note-takin' or journal keepin'," he preached, waving the frying pan for effect. "It's keepin' a blasted diary, for heaven's sake. But writin' for a purpose means writin' for a reader. If no one will understand it or appreciate it but you, what's the good in that?"

He put the frying pan down and leaned over the counter toward me. "Nicky tells me you're a singer, is that so?"

I nodded.

He lowered his voice to a hoarse whisper, and for once he wasn't growling. "Well, if you're a singer, you know that singin' for yourself is just practicin'. It's when you sing for others, for better or for worse, that you're really movin' a message. Do ya see?"

I reached out my hand and patted Uncle Jacob on his flushed cheek. "You're right, Uncle Jacob," I whispered. "Maybe I'll let you read something of mine sometime."

"Hrumph," he snorted. "I might make ya sing for your supper."

Uncle Jacob fixed a festive dinner, complete with linen tablecloths and napkins and lobster tails with pools of melted butter. But it was hard for me to be grateful. Mom was acting like a schoolgirl, Mr. Harris's plastic niceness was grating on my nerves, Uncle Jacob was growling again, and Nick was—well, the mystery had simply worn off.

I knew now that the air of polish and sophistication around Nick wasn't even skin-deep. As soon as we had arrived at the beach house, he jumped into the hall bathroom, changed

143

into his bathing suit, and ran out to the beach with his surfboard. He stayed out there until dinner time, riding the waves and not hesitating at all to flirt with whatever girl walked by.

The worst part was when I went into the bathroom and found his clothes, including his underwear, smack in the middle of the bathroom floor. "Good grief," I muttered, stepping carefully over his mess. "He's worse than Max."

So even though at dinner Nick was charming and polite, I ignored him. I had been so stupid to ever think I could—or would want to—be his girlfriend.

As I watched Mom and Mr. Harris talking I thought about what I wanted in a boyfriend. Someone who was honest. Someone who was real, and nice, and not a jerk. Someone who would listen to me when I had a problem and could give good advice. Someone who would talk to me when *he* had a problem.

Someone like Chip.

18

I took Suki for a walk after dinner. The beach was nice when the crowds of sun worshipers had gone home. The only people on the beach now were those lucky enough to live there. Suki chased a few sea gulls, then settled down happily to walk next to me.

I tried practicing my songs as I walked. It was easy to sing loud on the beach because no one could hear me over the pounding of the surf. Even the wind covered me up by catching my song and flinging it far away from me. But I couldn't do the flutey parts of "Villanelle" as I walked because I was too winded.

"I sure hope I don't have to do an encore," I told Suki, who probably couldn't hear me and certainly didn't care. "That song will kill any chance I might have."

The sun sank over the western horizon before

I knew what had happened, and I turned around to walk back. The sea at night is strange. I could sense the power of the waves and the vastness of the ocean, and I could almost feel the blackness of the air that surrounds both sand and sea. It was as though I were walking in moist velvet, and I couldn't hear anything of civilization. As I walked back, half-pulling my tired dog with me, I began to feel a little scared.

I finally found our beach house, at least it looked like ours from the outside. But as I walked up, I could see two shadowy figures sitting on the porch swing, and those figures were definitely kissing. Really kissing. This couldn't be our house, so I started to tiptoe away. Suki whined, though, and I took a second look. I recognized the red blouse my mom had worn at dinner. It was my mother and Tom Harris.

I felt sick, and for an instant I thought I'd throw up, right there on the sand. I let go of Suki's leash, knowing she'd go on in, while I turned and ran down the beach.

I hadn't gone ten steps into the darkness when a huge figure lunged at me. I screamed, then heard, "Confound it, missy, shut your mouth. Do ya want someone to call the cops?"

I stopped screaming, but stood there shaking as Uncle Jacob held my shoulders. "I only wanted to stop ya from running all the way to Miami," he hollered above the noise of waves and wind. "Can you calm down now?"

"You scared me," I yelled. "You scared me to death."

"I'm sorry," he yelled back. "Come on, a young girl like you's got no business out here after dark."

We walked up toward the beach house, with Uncle Jacob singing "Jimmy Crack Corn" loudly enough so that Mom and Tom Harris weren't kissing when we came up the porch steps. From the light that shone through the window, though, I could see that Mom's face was flushed and her eyes were glowing. I pushed past Uncle Jacob and let the screen door slam.

"Whaddya actin' rude for?" Jacob asked, coming in behind me. "It's not their fault. People are allowed to fall in love, ya know, even if they forget to prepare their kids for what's comin'."

"My mother isn't falling in love," I snapped, plopping down onto the couch. "She's just dating him to get back at my dad. I think she's just swept away because Tom's rich and money's been tight at our house lately."

"I don't know about that," Uncle Jacob muttered, settling back into a recliner. "I've seen Tom go out with quite a few women since Nick's mother passed on. I think his relationship with Claire is something special."

I made a face, but didn't feel like arguing.

"Have you tried lookin' at it from your mom's point of view?" Uncle Jacob asked, searching in his pocket for his cigar. He found it and rested it between his lips. "She's a lovely woman, and she needs companionship. Love, even."

I shook my head. "She has me. She has Max. She even has my father, and I think he's been missing her lately. We don't need Tom Harris."

"Maybe you don't and maybe she does," Uncle Jacob said. "But why don't you trust your mom to figure it all out?"

19

When we got home on Sunday afternoon,
the first thing I did was call Chip. I didn't usually
call guys, but this call couldn't wait. If I didn't
call, I probably wouldn't see him until school
started. But if all went well on Saturday, and
I went to the Spa next year, I might never see
Chip again.

I imagined us bumping into each other in
ten years. We'd be in the neighborhood grocery
store, twenty-three years old, engaged to other
people, or worse yet, already married. "Hi,
remember me?" I'd say. "I'm a famous singer
now."

"Cassie Perkins!" he'd smile and nod. "Of
course! You probably don't remember, but I had
a tremendous crush on you in eighth grade.
Now, of course, I'm marrying Andrea, but . . ."

"Hello?"

"Chip?"

"Cassie?"

I took a deep breath: "I want to apologize for that night at the mall when everything went so wrong. I could have made things easier for everyone, but I didn't, and I'm sorry. Now that you and Andrea are going out, I just wanted you to know that I appreciate you as a friend and hope you won't be mad at me forever. Good luck with your life."

"What?"

Hadn't he heard me? Didn't he understand?

"What do you mean, I'm going out with Andrea?"

"You're *not* going out with Andrea?"

"Not that I know of."

"But she said—" I tried to remember exactly what she had said. "She said you called her. A lot."

"I did, for a while. But all we ever talked about was you."

"Oh." Boy, did I feel dumb.

"Thanks for the apology. It's OK."

"Good." My thoughts were still spinning around. "Are you sure you're not going with Andrea?"

"No, I'm not." Chip began to laugh. "I haven't had time to go with anybody."

"Then—" I choked on the words. "We're still friends? You and me?"

"I guess we are." I could hear a smile in his voice.

"Thank goodness." I curled up on my bed, and we began to talk about all the things I couldn't tell anyone else: about Max, Dad, Mom, Tom Harris, the auditions, my frustrations, and Mr. Williams and his honeymoon. I even told Chip about Nick and the underwear on the floor. "He's just a kid," I laughed. "A kid in a prep school sweater."

"Nick's OK," Chip added generously. "I liked him." He paused a moment. "Cassie, if you're not doing anything tonight, why don't you come with me to the Main Event?"

"What's that?"

"It's an activity for the youth at our church," Chip explained. "My dad and I will pick you up."

"I'm sure it'd be OK," I said, knowing my mom was in such a good mood she'd agree to anything. "See you in a little while."

There were about twenty kids at the Main Event, which turned out to be a meeting in the youth pastor's home. When we arrived, the youth pastor's wife, Jane, gave each of us a little envelope and told us to write our names on the outside but not to peek inside.

We held onto our envelopes and played a few games. I knew a few of the kids from school and was surprised to see other kids there from Cocoa Beach, Cocoa, and Merritt Island, our rival schools. But there was no rivalry here. The youth pastor, Doug Richlett, had a smile for everyone, and we all had a good time together.

Doug asked us to sit down, so we did,

completely filling his living room. Chip made sure I had a good seat on a footstool, then he sat on the floor by me.

"I want you to pretend that your little envelope symbolizes your life," Doug said. "What things would you want to fill your envelope?"

He held up a poster board on which he had cut out little geometric symbols: a triangle, a square, a diamond. On these were written things such as *beauty, wealth, love, health, happiness,* and *maturity.* A few symbols were left blank.

A couple of kids mentioned *happiness* and *love.* One red-haired boy raised his hand and said, "Money, man, bucks! That's what I want!"

I rolled my eyes. I'd seen what money could do to people. It spoiled them into thinking they could do anything. "I'd want a true friend," I volunteered, pointing to a blank symbol. "Could I write that in?"

Doug's eyes lit up. "That's very good, Cassie," he said. "Most people go through life without more than a couple of true friends."

"I'd want fulfillment," another girl said. "I want to meet my goals."

Doug smiled. "That's important, too. You see, most people spend their entire life searching for all these things without really understanding what they need to make their life complete. Now open your envelopes."

We opened our envelopes, and from them we pulled out small hearts made from red construction paper. But in the center of each of them, someone had cut a hole in the shape of a cross.

"Most people don't realize that what they're really missing is Jesus Christ," Doug said, pointing to the cross-shaped void in his paper heart. "All the things you've mentioned—a true friend, fulfillment, joy, peace, and love—come from Jesus. When you allow him to meet these needs in your life, he leads you to places where you can discover whether or not it is his will for you to have the other things, too."

"Like health and wealth?" the red-haired boy joked.

Doug nodded. "Like health and wealth. But when Christ is leading your life, you leave those things up to him. They aren't your priority."

Jane came in then, carrying a tray of home-baked cookies. "Before we eat," Doug said, raising his hand so the boys wouldn't stampede to get at the food, "does anybody have any prayer requests for the coming week?"

Several kids raised their hands and mentioned sick parents or grandparents, and a couple of others said they'd be leaving on vacation soon. I thought about Max and Dad on the road and timidly raised my hand. "My brother and dad are traveling for the next few weeks," I said, and then, almost before I realized it, I added what was *really* on my mind. "And I have a big audition next Saturday. It's really important."

"OK, Cassie." Doug nodded. He lowered his head and started talking to God as if he were in

153

the room, perhaps just out of sight around the corner. "And Father, you know what's best for Cassie," Doug said, and at the mention of my name, I snapped to attention. "Show her your will and give her your peace. Keep her father and brother safe, too. Thank you, Father, for loving us. Amen."

Doug raised his head and the boys ran for the cookies. All except Chip, who looked up at me from the floor.

We went into the kitchen to talk. Jane was in there, puttering around with the dishes, but I didn't mind and neither did Chip. "Cassie, have you ever asked Jesus Christ to be the Lord of your life?" he asked.

"No." I answered, shaking my head. "I believe in God, though, and I've prayed to him. Remember *Oklahoma?* I prayed he'd get me through that."

"If you really want a forever friend, there's no better one than Jesus," Chip said. "No human being could ever compare." He smiled shyly. "Not even me."

"OK." I hesitated. "How do I do it?"

Chip shrugged. "Some people like to pray a prayer, and others simply make a decision. But it's something you do, not just something you think or feel."

So there in the kitchen, with Jane tiptoeing around us, I made the deal of my life. I gave my life to God and trusted him to figure it all out.

20

The night before my audition I sat on my bed and sang through "I Enjoy Being a Girl" in my head about a hundred times. I was afraid to really sing it as much as I wanted to because I was sure I'd wear out my voice. I'd die if I woke up with laryngitis.

But on Saturday morning I woke up and for once, everything was fine. I said a quick prayer under my breath to thank God.

I ate a good breakfast, mainly because I knew I'd be too nervous to eat lunch with my audition set for two o'clock. The phone rang at ten; it was Chip.

"I can come to your audition, right?" he asked. "And Andrea, too. We both want to be there to cheer you on."

"Thanks," I said. "I could use the moral support."

"We'll be there," Chip promised.

"Chip?"

"Yeah?"

"Since I gave my life to Christ, does this mean he's going to arrange it so I win the audition?"

Chip hesitated. "Is that the only reason you did it? So you could win?"

"No." I meant it. "Not at all."

"Well, then, the Lord will work everything out as best for you. You should give him your best effort and then leave everything to him."

"OK." That sounded good. All I had to do was follow and do my best. That was even a relief—I had been looking for someone to lead me for a long time.

We hung up, and I went to the piano and checked my audition schedule again just to be sure I hadn't misread it. It would be terrible to show up at the wrong place or at the wrong time. The auditions were going on all day, and the morning session had begun at nine and would end at noon. The judges would break for lunch and resume at one-thirty. I had to be there at one-thirty because the judges didn't want any interruptions, and if they were ahead of schedule, they wanted to move ahead.

I mentally sang through "I Enjoy Being a Girl" again, adding the motions and steps. I rechecked my outfit: Mom and I had decided on her frilly lace blouse and a straight black skirt. It was frilly enough for "I Enjoy Being a Girl," and yet serious enough if I had to sing "Villanelle."

But I was confident I'd wow 'em on the first

song. The phone rang and Mom answered it; after a few minutes she stuck her head into my room: "I have a message for you: 'Knock 'em dead.'"

"Who from?" I stiffened. "Tom Harris?"

"No," Mom said, shaking her head. "Uncle Jacob."

I couldn't help smiling. It was a good feeling to know Uncle Jacob was thinking of me.

At noon, I climbed in my bubble bath for a ten-minute soak. Mom rapped on the bathroom door and put a box of long-stemmed roses by the sink. I peeked out from behind the shower curtain and looked at the roses suspiciously. "Who are they from?"

I was afraid they'd be from Tom, that he'd be trying to buy my affection as obviously as he'd tried to buy my way into the Spa. But Mom read the card: "For the original Wild Irish Rose. Break a leg, Gypsy Girl. Love, Dad."

I sank all the way under the bubbles in complete happiness.

At one-thirty, right on schedule, I crept into the darkened theater at the Spa with Chip, Andrea, and Mom. I think Mr. Harris had wanted to come, but Mom discouraged him. We chose seats toward the back, and I settled into the plush velour theater seat while my stomach felt as up-and-down as the spring-up chair I was in.

A tall, skinny kid that I remembered from the orientation meeting stood up, handed his music to the accompanist at the gleaming black grand piano, and walked to the center of the stage. He was as stiff as cardboard, but he announced, "I'd like to sing 'Still wie die Nacht' by Carl Bohm."

"German?" Chip whispered.

I nodded. "I think so."

The boy sang, nervously and timidly. On one high note, his voice cracked.

Chip groaned. "I feel sorry for him," he whispered.

I ached for him, too. And for me, because although my voice probably wouldn't crack because of puberty, it was likely to crack, squeak, or completely fail from nerves. Or, more likely, I'd stand up there and forget every word.

The boy finished and waited a moment to see if the judges would want to hear another song. "Thank you very much," Mrs. Allan said, not even looking up. "That's all we need to hear."

The boy took his music from the accompanist and slunk off the stage.

"Next," Mrs. Allan called, "is Shalisa McRay."

I hadn't noticed her in the dark theater, but Shalisa sprang out of a seat down front. "Hello, Mrs. Allan," she chirped, "and good afternoon, Mr. Hanson, Mrs. Miniver." She nodded to each of them.

"Look at her," I whispered to Andrea. "She doesn't have a nervous bone in her body."

Andrea only shook her head in disbelief. "I hope, for your sake, Cassie, that she's competing for a tenth grade slot."

"No," I whispered. "She's in ninth grade, same as us. And because of her connections, she's got it made."

"Don't worry," Chip said. "Maybe she can't sing at all."

Shalisa gracefully climbed the steps to the stage, the stage lights gleaming off her golden hair. She gave her music to the pianist, exchanged a few chummy words with him, and practically floated to center stage. She assumed a position and nodded to the accompanist.

He began to play familiar music, and I groaned. Sure enough, the song was "I Enjoy Being a Girl," and when Shalisa sang it, she was a girl to the thousandth degree, a girl without equal, a girl . . . "sui generis," I whispered to Andrea.

"Huh?" She whispered back. "What's that?"

"It's one of Max's words," I explained. "It means without equal, top of the line."

Shalisa gave a flawless performance. She *lived* the song. Singing it was as natural to her as breathing. She made every motion, every note, every phrase, seem effortless.

I was doomed to fail. I couldn't follow her performance. I couldn't top it or even equal it. But, strangely enough, I wasn't devastated.

When Shalisa finished, the judges actually applauded. "Do you have another treat for us, dear?" Mrs. Allan crooned, and Shalisa launched into the sad but sweet "Memory" from the musical *Cats*.

159

"Well, that's it," I whispered to my friends. "There's no way I can compare to that. She was good; in fact, she was better than me. My best won't even compare to her."

"You can't just give up," Chip said. "You haven't even tried yet."

"I'm just being realistic, Chip."

"What about the other song?" Mom spoke up. "That song about the birds? It's very different, and nothing like Shalisa's. Your voice is different than hers, honey, and it is well-suited for that bird song."

"What's the bird song?" Andrea crinkled her nose. "I've never heard of it."

"You won't ever hear of it, either," I laughed. "It's not exactly top forty material."

As I suspected, my name was called next. I left the music for "I Enjoy Being a Girl" in my seat and clutched the copy of "Villanelle." It was the hardest song I'd ever tried to learn, but now it was all or nothing. If I pulled it off, it'd be great, probably worthy of a scholarship. If I blew it, they'd laugh me off the stage. All my dreams depended on this song.

"I'd like to sing 'Villanelle,' by Eva Dell Acqua," I told the judges. I walked to center stage and was embarrassed by how loudly my shoes clunked across the floor. I took a breath, then nodded to the accompanist.

The piano began the rippling introduction, and I looked down at the wooden floor of the stage. Strange thoughts flitted through my mind: Uncle Jacob and "Jimmy Crack Corn," the first words, "Swiftly the swallows are flying," and Max and his tube of toothpaste. How worn the floor was! What would happen if I just stood and stared at the floor? But the music continued on, and abruptly, I knew it was time to sing.

I took a deep breath and began.

One month later, Mom brought in the mail and handed me an envelope from the Central Florida School for Performing Arts. I opened it:

> Dear Miss Perkins:
>
> We are pleased to inform you that you have qualified for admission to our school and the next fall term. Your application has been filed, and registration will begin on August 20. Due to our financial structure, your full tuition payment for the semester will be due at registration.
>
> We look forward to having you with us.
>
> Sincerely,
> (Mrs.) Janette Allan

"Well?" Mom looked at me.

I tossed the letter on the counter. "I passed the entrance audition."

"Congratulations, honey." Mom patted my back and peeked at the letter. "Nothing about the scholarship?"

"Nothing." I was tempted to throw the letter

away. After all, registration would begin next week, so surely they would have let me know about the scholarship by now. They could have even telephoned.

But I was surprised at how calm I was. A chance to go to school at the Spa would have been a chance to develop a talent I loved. But if it didn't work out, well, I had done my best and taken my chance like God wanted me to. If he was really running things, it was his move now.

Dad and Max pulled back into town that afternoon and stopped at our house. "The trip was great," Max said, after showing me his briefcase stuffed with souvenirs, "but we were thinking of you a lot. Did your audition go OK?"

I nodded. "It went great. I didn't faint or squeak or anything. I even passed the audition, but I haven't heard anything about the scholarship." I shrugged. "So if I don't hear anything in a couple of days, I guess I didn't get it."

Max's brown eyes were shining. "You can have my money, Cassie," he said. "If it means that much to you."

I rumpled his hair. "No, kiddo, that's your dream. I don't want to take it from you. It's OK, I'm trusting someone to work everything out."

Max gave me a funny look, but Dad came into the room holding the pile of mail Mom had accumulated for him. "Want to keep Max here for a while?" he teased.

"Sure," I said. "It's too quiet around here without him."

"Well, I've got to pick up my mail at the condo and then report back to work," Dad said, idly flipping through the stack of magazines and letters. "But it'll probably be mostly junk mail like this."

He pulled out a copy of *National Geographic*. "Here, Max, since you're staying here you might as well keep this." Dad tossed the magazine through the air to Max, and as it flipped end over end, a long envelope flew out of its pages.

The envelope landed at my feet. It was from the School for Performing Arts.

"Cassie?" Mom asked. "Is that your letter?"

I picked it up and held it for a minute. "Well . . ." I looked up at Dad, Max, and Mom. "I guess I'll know something now, won't I?" I tore the end off the envelope and slid the letter out. But before I read it, I looked again at my family. "I want you all to know that I'm OK," I said. "Whatever happens, it's going to be the best thing for me."

I began reading aloud: "Dear Miss Perkins, it is with great pleasure that we, the scholarship committee, announce that you have been awarded the Constance Hamilton Scholarship for Potential Growth and Achievement."

"That's wonderful!" Mom squealed.

"Congratulations, Cass," Max said.

"Way to go, gypsy girl."

I kept on reading. "The scholarship will be renewed each fall for four years, or until you complete your education at the Central Florida School for Performance Arts. Congratulations

163

on your fine achievement. Sincerely, Mrs. Janette Allan."

Max didn't seem very surprised. "So who was Constance Hamilton?" he asked.

"I don't know." I let out a little squeak of joy. "But I love her!"

"I'm thrilled for you," Dad said, smiling proudly.

Mom gave me a hug. "And you did it all yourself," she whispered. "Nobody handed it to you; you earned it."

I thought of Chip, who had helped me see that there were more important things than winning a contest. He had helped me fill the biggest hole in my life. And God had given me peace about whatever happened. He was leading me.

"I didn't do it all myself," I said, smiling. "I had help from a couple of true friends."